# P
## LUVES
# DEVON
## CRAZY CREAM ADVENTURES

## GILLIAN YOUNG

Copyright © 2022 Gillian Young

The moral right of the author has been asserted.

Apart from any fair dealing for the purposes of research or private study,
or criticism or review, as permitted under the Copyright, Designs and Patents
Act 1988, this publication may only be reproduced, stored or transmitted, in
any form or by any means, with the prior permission in writing of the
publishers, or in the case of reprographic reproduction in accordance with
the terms of licences issued by the Copyright Licensing Agency. Enquiries
concerning reproduction outside those terms should be sent to the publishers.

This is a work of fiction. Names, characters, businesses, places, events
and incidents are either the products of the author's imagination
or used in a fictitious manner. Any resemblance to actual persons,
living or dead, or actual events is purely coincidental.

*To my parents, with love x*

# SUMMER HOLIDAY

Poppy, the crazy cream retriever, trotted down the hall, her tail wagging, nose twitching and stomach grumbling. *What was that smell? It was delicious!* By the time she reached the living room, she had recognised the tantalising tasty aroma of one of her many favourite things – toast.

She stopped in the doorway and looked around. She lifted her chin and sniffed the air. She licked her lips, lapping up the drool that was already forming around her jowls.

No one seemed to be about, even though she could hear them. Her family were busy getting their things

1

together. Mom and Dad were gathering their bags, mobile phones, camera and keys. Amidst the hustle and bustle, Poppy sensed everyone's excitement, and she felt it too.

Soon, they would be on the road to Devon, one of her favourite places – except for the forest, that is.

Every year the family spent a week on the Devonshire coast. Mom always said that the fresh sea air was good for everyone – and yes, that was true. But really, Poppy liked the ice cream parlours. Deliciously cool ice cream in an array of different flavours. Vanilla, raspberry, bubble gum, cookies and cream, and of course – her favourite – strawberry.

At the thought of food, Poppy curled her tongue around another string of slobber swinging from her jowls. She stared at the plate of hot buttered toast sitting on the coffee table just waiting to be eaten.

Poppy sat down and grunted.

She remembered all too clearly what had happened last time she helped herself to food from the table…

Back then, her family had been setting off for a day at the safari park – and what a fabulous day it had turned out to be. But it hadn't been the greatest start. Poppy's mouth watered as she thought back to that delicious bowl of ice cream – Dad's ice cream – that had been left on the table. How could she resist? Then she remembered Dad walking in and finding the empty bowl. Seeing how unhappy he was had made her feel miserable.

Never again would she help herself to food that was not in her bowl.

'Is that all the bags?' Mom called from in the kitchen.

Poppy looked over her shoulder and saw Dad walking past carrying a large bag and pulling an even bigger suitcase behind him.

'I hope so,' he said, breathing heavily.

Poppy trotted after him. She made her parent – or pawrent, as she liked to call her mom and dad – laugh by growling and howling at him.

'Won't be long now, Poppy,' he said.

Beads of sweat glistened on Dad's brow as he heaved the bag off his shoulder and let go of the bulging case. He stood rubbing where the strap had been.

'We're only going for a week,' he grumbled, but seeing Poppy, he smiled and winked. 'We'll soon be back on that beach, Pop.' He leaned down and rubbed her chin.

Poppy licked his hand, her tail wagging with excitement. She loved the beach. All that sand to dig, dig and dig. One of these days she was going to reach the bottom of that giant sandpit.

She glanced over at the small sandpit in the garden, the one little Evie still loved to play in. Evie was her human sister and one of her favourite playmates. The other was Jack, her human brother.

Poppy spotted one of Jack's footballs in the sandpit and another beside the tree. He'd discovered a new passion – football Poppy loved playing this game with

Jack and Dad. She had a feeling, though, that sometimes they didn't appreciate her stealing the ball. But it was fun being chased by them while holding the ball in her mouth.

Two pigeons swooped down and landed in the sandpit. Poppy's heart raced. She loved chasing pigeons. She growled softly then set off at full pelt, barking excitedly. The pigeons didn't move. Poppy was getting closer and closer.

*Oh my word, I'm actually going to catch them!*

Her excitement spilt over into a succession of deep barks. But just as she was within leaping distance, the birds took off, teasingly slow but still out of Poppy's reach.

She stopped. Tongue out. Panting. Her tail fell still. But then her nose twitched. She knew that smell. She turned just in time to see a rabbit racing across the lawn.

'Wait!' she barked, starting to run again. 'Wait a minute!'

The rabbit disappeared through a small hole in the hedge.

Poppy grumbled at the hedge. She sniffed, pressing her nose against the hole, wishing she was small enough to squeeze through it. She tried digging around the hole. Yet try as she might, she just couldn't squeeze through. She pressed her nose through the gap and then she heard Dad's voice.

'Aye! Stop that!'

Slowly, Poppy stepped back and looked over her shoulder. Dad had loaded the bags into the car and was now watching her.

She was about to walk over to him when she heard a scratching sound and the soft thud of something landing not too far away. Poppy turned. There, peering down at her, was Boxer, the pub's cat.

The White Stag pub and restaurant was only a few doors down from their house. Her family went there to celebrate special occasions like birthdays and Christmas. Poppy had been there many, many times.

The White Stag was a large place with a cool tiled floor that was nice for sitting on during hot summer days. It also had thick wooden beams running from floor to ceiling that Poppy would have loved to sink her teeth into. But what she loved most of all was when the landlady gave her a bowl filled with meat from the day's carvery. Roasted beef, lamb, turkey or chicken.

Boxer, the White Stag's cat, liked to wander into Poppy's garden all the time. Poppy wouldn't have minded if the cat came to play, but he didn't. Boxer was a tease, a big, grey and white tease. He'd march into her garden and roll on to his back, showing off his super-huge white feet.

Poppy wished that just one of these animals, who had the cheek to trespass on her turf, would play with her from time to time. But, like all the others, Boxer was never any fun. Every time he lay on his back, Poppy trotted over. Sometimes she'd run, other days she'd creep up to him. But Boxer always heard her and jumped out of reach – or would take a swipe at her with one of his huge white paws.

*Rude.*

Now, here he was again, peering down at Poppy from the top of the fence.

'I suppose you're going to run away again?' Poppy barked.

Boxer stared at her with his big, pale green eyes.

Poppy stared back.

*Why didn't he run? Could it be that Boxer finally wanted to play?*

Poppy wagged her tail. She barked happily.

But as soon as she jumped up against the fence, her weight making the panel sway and creak, Boxer arched his back. He hissed at her then turned tail and leapt off the ridge and into the field behind.

Poppy stood up against the fence, staring at the now empty space where Boxer had been.

She whined, imagining the rabbit, and now the cat, having a fantastic game together in that field – the one she couldn't get into.

'Are we ready?' Poppy heard Mom say.

'Yes, I was just watching Poppy,' Dad called back.

'Let me guess, was she chasing the rabbits again?'

Poppy heard the laughter in Dad's voice as he said, 'And the pigeons, and Boxer. Honestly, Jane, Poppy needs a playmate.'

Poppy spun round.

*A playmate? Share my family? Not likely!*

She raced over to them.

'I've already got my playmates, thank you very much,' she barked as Dad opened the car door. She leapt inside, landing in between Jack and Evie.

First she licked Jack's hand, then Evie's, happy to have two of the best buddies she could wish for. Yet, there had been another, someone she missed very much.

Harley.

Poppy sighed, thinking back and wondering about her little furriend. What adventures they'd had around the safari park! How she'd worried about him. Protected him. The fun they'd had together. Yet, she doubted her little furriend was that little anymore. Maybe he'd be the one protecting her – if only they could meet up again.

She rested her head against Evie's shoulder – much to her little sister's delight.

'Come on then, let's go,' Mom said, settling into the car and fastening her seatbelt.

Dad climbed in. He turned in his seat and grinned at Jack, Evie and Poppy.

'Are we all buckled up?'

'Yes,' said Jack and Evie.

'Is Poppy all buckled up?'

'Yes.'

'Right then, off we go.'

Dad started the engine. The children chattered excitedly as the car turned out of the driveway.

Poppy looked out of the back window, watching their house disappear into the distance.

'Devon, here we come!' Poppy howled.

# SINKING PAWS AND WET SAND

Poppy recognised the smell of the beach, as it drifted through the open window. It was clear, fresh, salty and cool, with the light scent of chips, ice cream, candyfloss and burgers.

She stepped over Evie and pressed her nose against the window. As they drove past the small café and burger bar, she licked her lips. She knew these places well, they'd been there many times before. This could mean only one thing…

They had arrived. They were in Devon.

'Devon! Devon!' Poppy barked. She stood up, pushing Evie to one side and batting her little sister's face with her tail.

'Well, that was the quickest drive on record,' Mom said.

'That's because we set off in good time,' Dad replied, unbuckling his seatbelt.

Poppy heard the surprise in Dad's voice. It was rare that the Robinson family set off anywhere on time. There was usually something to hold them up, something that had been forgotten, an unexpected phone call or an urgent visit to the toilet; but not this time.

Mom glanced at her watch then looked at Dad.

'So, what are we going to do for the next three hours? We can't get into the cottage until three o'clock.'

Poppy stared at the sand that stretched out as far as she could see. Dogs raced across the beach chasing footballs, frisbees, tennis balls or just racing for the fun of it. She longed to do the same, to stretch her legs and feel the air rushing through her fur.

'Come on, Poppy,' Jack said, then paused before opening the door. 'Where's my football?'

Poppy threw her head back and howled. *This day couldn't get any better!* She looked at Jack and groan-growled, 'Hurry up!'

Just as she leapt out of the car she could have sworn she heard Mom say, 'I wonder if we'll manage to coax Poppy into the sea this time.'

Then, Dad replied, 'By the end of this holiday, she'll love the sea – you mark my words.'

Poppy grunted. Surely she'd misheard. There was

no possibility whatsoever that she and the sea could be friends. Absolutely. No way.

The minute everyone was out of the car, Poppy began to run alongside Jack and Evie, leaving Mom and Dad trailing behind carrying towels and bags.

They settled beside a giant rock. Mom laid a bath towel out on the sand then relaxed with her camera.

'Our first photo of the holiday,' she said.

Evie and Jack groaned, but Poppy knew they were only playing. Every time they went out Mom took hundreds of photos. Poppy had once heard Dad joke that it was a family tradition.

'OK, but hurry up,' Dad said, standing with Jack and Evie and glancing around to check if anyone was looking.

Meanwhile, Poppy decided to check out the exciting new sights and smells. She walked past her family, who were lined up, all grinning and waiting for Mom to take the picture. With her nose pressed into the sand, she could smell a thousand things: fish, seaweed, salt, seagulls, other dogs –big, small, stocky and thin – and even the hint of chips and spilt fruit drinks.

She snorted. She grunted. Her bottom and tail swayed from side to side. She was lost in her own world of smells until Dad took her by the collar.

'Come here, you,' he said, gently drawing her beside him. 'You're in on the photo too.'

Poppy knew what to do. To play along meant less time wasted, so she sat up, stuck her chest out, lifted her chin and waited.

'Perfect!' Mom grinned.

'Can we go now?' Evie moaned.

'Yes, can we?' Poppy whined.

'Yes, yes,' Mom said.

Shoes and socks were thrown off. For a second, Poppy was tempted to steal one of them. She loved socks. She loved to chew them until they were wet and smelt doggy. But there were too many other distractions out on the beach – far more tempting than socks.

She barked and raced across the sand with Dad, Jack and Evie. She darted after the ball as Dad and Jack kicked it to each other. Occasionally, a dog grabbed her attention but, as though reading her mind, Dad drew her back by calling her name.

Evie skipped along beside them. Poppy jumped up and down, trying to skip like her sister. Poppy lunged and dived for the ball as it was kicked from Dad to Jack, from Jack to Dad. She was having the best time.

Then she felt it. Cold water rushing over her paws. Backwards and forwards. Backwards and forwards. The sand felt strange – her paws were sinking into the ground!

Poppy leapt backwards. She lowered her head and barked. She barked again. And again. She'd forgotten about the water that rolled, rumbled and whooshed. She shook, remembering the last encounter.

It had been a year ago. Dad had coaxed her in with a biscuit. How could she refuse? Then, all of a sudden, water rolled towards her. It washed over her, around and back again before coming for her once more with a loud whoosh. She remembered stumbling, her soaking fur stuck to her body, the taste of salt on her tongue.

Poppy shuddered at the memory. Never would she venture into the water again.

She barked at the sea. 'Back off. Go away. Leave me alone.'

But still, the waves came. She jumped backwards, her paws only narrowly missing the water – and the seaweed that floated on the surface. The seaweed edged closer and closer, like wiggling dark fingers, reaching out, ready to wrap themselves around her legs.

Then she felt a small hand on her back. She turned and saw Evie. She smiled at Poppy and leaned in closer.

'It's OK, Poppy. It's only the sea.'

'Only the sea?' Poppy growled.

'Come on. Retrievers are supposed to like water,' Jack shouted. But he wasn't cross, Poppy could see he was smiling. Then he bent forward and splashed her.

Poppy scrunched her eyes and jumped backwards. She didn't like this, not one bit. She spun around, ready to turn tail and run back to Mom – but then she saw him…

# SAMSON

Poppy froze. Only her eyes moved, following the handsome border collie as he ran through the waves.

*I wish I could move like that*, she thought, wishing just then that she wasn't so heavy and clumsy. The rustling and whooshing of the sea didn't bother him, neither did the seaweed floating around his legs. With his head held high, he ran beside his owner, eyes fixed on her and no one else.

The girl jogged through the water at a pace the collie matched easily. Her long dark hair flew behind her shoulders. Occasionally she glanced down at the collie and smiled. For one insane moment, Poppy felt jealous. Jealous that a dog like him would look up at his owner like that.

Poppy whined. *I wish he'd look at me that way.*

As the sea rose and fell, he leapt higher, gracefully, athletically. He seemed to dance across the surface.

Suddenly a spray of water covered Poppy from head to tail. She scrunched her eyes and jumped backwards. All thoughts of the girl and her handsome dog vanished as she was splashed again and again.

She barked. 'Stop that!'

She spun around, lowered her head and barked and growled.

'Come on, Poppy,' Dad said, laughing. 'This is what you need. It'll cool you down.'

A Jack Russell dog bounced through the waves towards her.

'What's your problem? It won't hurt you, you know,' it barked whilst jumping around her.

'I don't care,' Poppy answered.

'Just follow me.'

'Nope.'

'Are you scared?'

'Nope. I just don't like the sea.'

Someone whistled. The Jack Russell turned and ran away.

Poppy took a deep breath, glad that the little dog had gone.

'You're not scared, are you?' came a deep, gruff bark from beside her.

Poppy sighed. She turned and saw a large black Labrador staring at her.

'No, I just don't like water.'

The Labrador howled. 'A retriever that doesn't like water! I've heard it all now.'

Poppy couldn't see what was funny. All she knew was that her paws were wet, the sand was sinking between her claws and she just wanted to get back to Mom – back to dry land and to lie out on the big, dry towel.

'Relax,' the Labrador continued. 'It's fun and the water's nice and cool.'

Dad was calling her to him. She was pleased by the distraction. But the problem was he stood knee-deep in the sea.

'Come on, Poppy. Come here, girl.' Dad bent over and scooped the water up in his hands, then threw it in her direction.

She grumbled and groaned. She took a step back.

'No way,' Poppy growled.

The Labrador soon got bored and raced back to his owners who were even farther out to sea. Poppy concluded that everyone must be mad. There was no way she was following Dad, no way she was going to '*just relax*' and absolutely no way was she going to swallow more of that horrible seawater.

Poppy would rather be hot and bothered than wet and that applied to paddling pools, puddles and – heaven forbid – bath time. She turned, hearing Evie and Jack running towards her, their feet splashing through the sea as they went.

Poppy turned tail and ran. With her heart racing, she didn't have time to think. She spun around and collided, headlong with – she had no idea what.

The shock unsteadied her and she stumbled. She tasted the salty water again; she felt it in her eyes and her ears. She managed to steady herself in time, narrowly avoiding falling head over paws. Then she froze. She wished the wet sand would swallow her up. Of all the things to bump into…

The border collie glared down at her.

Her heart sank seeing the angry look in his eyes. Instead of the proud look he had given his owner, the collie curled his lip and snarled.

Poppy whined. 'I'm sorry. I-I didn't see you.'

But the collie only growled louder.

Poppy gulped. She didn't know what to do.

To her relief, Dad, Jack and Evie appeared beside her. Dad held on to her collar while Evie stroked her back.

'I'm so sorry!' The collie's owner jogged towards them, her cheeks flushed. 'Samson. Come here.'

Samson – the handsome collie dog – spun around and ran to her.

Despite running on such a warm and sunny day, the girl didn't seem hot and tired. She combed her hand through her long hair and smiled.

'No need to apologise,' Dad said, 'It was Poppy who bumped into your dog.'

To Poppy's dismay, Samson ignored her. He only had eyes for the girl. She watched the collie and his owner jog away across the shore.

'Come on,' Dad said. Poppy could hear the dejection in his voice. Now her family were disappointed in her too.

Sometimes she wished she was less clumsy and more agile, like Samson. Yet, the sea hadn't helped. In Poppy's opinion, the sight and sound of those waves were enough to make any dog skittish. Funny that Samson didn't mind, though – then again, she had never come across a dog like him before.

Poppy glared at the sea. 'It's all your fault,' she growled, then trudged after her family, and on to dry land.

# BUTTERCUP FARM

Mom stepped out of the car and swung open a large wooden gate. Dad steadily drove the car along the wide gravel driveway.

Poppy looked around. Everything smelled strange and new. She smelt the farm, the fresh country air and dust from the dry gravel as the car tyres crunched and popped over stones.

To Poppy's delight, she saw a large lawn – perfect for a game of football and perfect to race around when she'd stolen the ball from Dad and Jack. The lawn was edged on one side with large wooden posts supporting wire fencing which separated the garden from what lay beyond.

Behind the fencing were two black and white animals. They didn't have fur or feathers but unusual noses and short, curly tails. Poppy was mesmerised. She could hear them making grunting sounds. Even though she had no idea what they were saying, she had a feeling they were pleased to see the family arrive.

Dad stopped the car outside a stone cottage. One of the walls was painted cream, which hurt Poppy's eyes in the brilliant sunshine.

Mom walked over to them and opened the back door. As Jack climbed out, Poppy sat and waited patiently. Her tail smacked against the seat. She was excited and eager to get out and explore.

'Come on,' Mom said.

Poppy didn't need to be asked twice.

'Look, Mom!' Evie cried as she ran around the car and up to the long stretch of ranch fencing.

Poppy was curious. She trotted after Evie then stopped and jumped backwards. She barked, 'Who's that?'

A white animal stood on the other side of the fence. It was taller than her and had two large horns on the top of its head. But Poppy didn't feel threatened. She stood beside Evie and wagged her tail as the creature poked its nose between the wooden railings.

Mom reached over the fence and gently stroked the animal's muzzle.

'Hello there,' she said softly.

The creature looked at them and then made the strangest noise. Poppy tilted her head and whined.

Evie giggled. She wrapped her arm around Poppy's shoulders.

'She's saying hello, Poppy,' Mom chuckled. 'Don't worry, she won't hurt you, you big chicken.'

'Chicken? I'm not a chicken,' Poppy grumbled. 'For a start, I haven't got feathers. Even I know those birds over there are chickens. I'm a cream golden retriever and proud of it!'

'It's a goat!' Jack said, tucking his football under his arm and reaching out to let the goat nuzzle the palm of his hand.

Poppy watched the creature greet her family. It seemed friendly enough. Maybe it would like to play later? She trotted over to Dad. She growled and barked softly at him. 'I've made a new friend, look. It's called a goat.'

Dad slung a large bag over his shoulder and then pulled a suitcase from the car.

'Yes. Yes,' he said to her. 'I'll go and say hello to the animals later, but first things first.' He continued to pull the luggage out, one bag at a time.

Just as Jack walked over, ready to help his dad, Poppy noticed two people approaching. She wagged her tail.

*More friends!*

As they drew nearer, Poppy was certain she'd seen one of them before.

# THE BRIGGS FAMILY

'Hello! You must be the Robinson family,' said a lady with a warm and welcoming smile. Poppy liked her cheerful round face and rosy cheeks. She had a pair of sunglasses perched on the top of her head, nestled into her thick dark hair like a pair of big black eyes.

Mom and Dad walked over. They shook hands and then introduced the rest of the family. When Poppy heard her name, she trotted forward and pushed her nose into the lady's hand.

'Hello, gorgeous girl,' the friendly lady said. 'Welcome to Buttercup Farm.'

Poppy jumped up at her, making sure to give the nice lady her best goldie grin.

'Poppy, get down,' Dad said and gently held on to her collar.

'Oh, I don't mind.' The lady waved her hand towards the animals behind the fencing. 'I love animals, and you can't beat a warm welcome from a goldie, can you?' she said, leaning over and massaging Poppy's ears.

*I'm going to like it here*, Poppy decided as she licked the lady's hand.

'I'm Carol Briggs, and this is my daughter, Florence, but everyone calls her Flo.'

Flo smiled. She said hello as she tucked her hands into the back pockets of her jeans. Poppy was certain she'd seen the girl somewhere before.

'You'll meet my husband, Colin, later,' Carol said. 'He's out on the fields with the sheep at the moment. He's usually around the farm so if there's anything you need, just give either of us a call. Our house is just behind the cottage.'

Carol nodded towards the farmhouse. It was a tall stone building, its roof visible from behind the cottage.

Flo stepped forward. She crouched down in front of Poppy and smiled.

'Hello, Poppy. It's nice to meet you properly,' she said, then looked up at Dad. 'I'm sorry about earlier.'

Now Poppy knew where she'd seen her before. She was the girl on the beach with Samson, the border collie.

Poppy looked around, but to her disappointment, Samson was nowhere to be seen.

'Don't worry about it,' Dad said. 'We should be apologising. Poppy gets a bit bouncy at times.'

Poppy sighed. *That's Dad's polite way of saying I get over-excited and clumsy.*

'Oh dear,' said Carol. 'I can imagine Samson was rude. He can be a grump, I'm afraid.'

She looked at Poppy and winked before turning her attention to Evie.

'You must meet Oliver and Olive. Oliver's my French bulldog and Olive's a pug. They're much friendlier than Samson.'

Evie's face lit up as two small dogs appeared behind the fence.

'There they are, my babies,' Carol said, proudly.

Poppy walked over.

*More playmates!*

Oliver, the black French bulldog, wore a navy blue bow tie with white paw prints all over it. Olive, the pug, wore a similar bow tie in pink. Poppy thought they looked very stylish and wanted to tell them so.

As she stepped forward, one of the pugs' velvety black ears twitched. It snorted loudly, making Poppy jump. The two dogs exchanged looks and then grunted.

Poppy growled softly. 'I'm Poppy. Nice to meet you.'

Oliver and Olive narrowed their eyes – then belched in unison.

Poppy stared.

*What could she say to that?*

Carol seemed oblivious to her dogs' strange greeting. She walked up to Poppy and leaned over the fence.

'Evie, watch this,' she said and gazed down at the fawn and black pug. 'Olive, speak.'

Olive lifted her chin and barked.

Poppy was a little put out by this. *So the dogs do have manners,* she grumbled. *So why was I greeted with a burp?*

Oliver began shuffling and snuffling.

'OK. OK, now it's your turn,' Carol chuckled. 'Oliver, bow.'

The French bulldog leaned forward and lowered his head. Evie applauded. Poppy heard Mom and Dad gasp. She had to admit, she'd never seen anything like it before.

Yet, these two were more interested in the hoomans' attention than hers – which reminded her of Boxer, the big, unfriendly cat back home.

Poppy had seen enough. She stepped back and looked around. A large barn caught her eye. It stretched from the cottage to the gate. Yet it wasn't the barn that made her catch her breath. It was the tall trees behind – a forest. Forests were one of Poppy's favourite places in the world.

Back home, they lived opposite a huge wood called Childer's Forest. Her family took her there every day.

She loved zooming around the trees, eating mud, rolling in exquisite smells like fox pee and horse poo; and then there were the squirrels – she loved chasing them especially.

'Come on,' Carol said. 'I'll show you around the cottage.'

Poppy followed everyone inside.

First, Carol showed them Evie and Jack's bedroom, a large bathroom and her pawrents' room.

The Robinsons then followed Carol upstairs. Poppy's claws slipped and skidded against the polished wooden floor. She stood at the top and looked around the open-plan room. A small kitchen stood on one side and a cosy living area with two huge settees covered with plump cushions stood to the other.

Wooden beams crisscrossed above their heads, reminding Poppy of the branches that stretched from tree to tree in the forest back home. She turned and squinted against the dazzling sunlight that poured through the large windows. One of them had a view overlooking the front of the farmhouse. She noticed a small garden with hens and geese meandering to and fro. There was also a pond where a family of ducks swam happily.

She was just thinking how great it would be to chase them when she felt someone pat her head. She looked up and saw Carol smiling down at her.

'See you later, Poppy.' Carol walked downstairs and let herself out.

Poppy turned back to the window for another look at the farmhouse and garden. Two fluffy beanbags stood beside the doorstep. One was blue, the other pink. *It would be good to stretch out on those – if only they were not so small.* Poppy mused. She watched Oliver and Olive saunter up to their beds and flop down.

*That's the life.* Poppy wished she had a bed like that.

Suddenly, the serenity was shattered by a scream.

Poppy pulled her ears back. She looked left and right, her eyes wide open.

*What's happened? What's wrong?*

She jumped to her feet and raced downstairs towards the sound of the cries.

# BUTTERCUP

Poppy raced down the stairs. She could hear Mom and Dad's voices and found them standing in the bedroom. Poppy pushed in between them and looked around.

*What's happened? What's going on?*

Then she heard Evie giggling. Jack's eyes were sparkling as he held up a red and white Kentley Town FC football and shirt.

Meanwhile, Evie sat on her bed, cuddling a fluffy golden retriever puppy.

*So that's it,* Poppy realised with relief. Nothing was wrong after all. Jack and Evie had just had a visit from the Holiday Fairy.

The Fairy left them a present every holiday. One day, Poppy was determined to see her, just like she was resolute in seeing Father Christmas, the Easter Bunny and the Tooth Fairy.

'I'm going to call her Buttercup,' Evie said and kissed the cuddly puppy on the nose.

Jack laughed and ruffled the puppy's ear. 'Cute,' he said before turning back to his football goodies.

Poppy glared at Evie's present. Her initial relief knowing nothing was wrong was quickly replaced with displeasure.

'Another puppy? We don't need two dogs in this family!' she growled. 'Buttercup?' Poppy snorted, watching Evie kiss and cuddle the puppy dog. 'What kind of name is that? A buttercup's a flower, not a dog.' She looked away – conveniently forgetting that her own name was Poppy.

There was something about that puppy she didn't like. Poppy wasn't sure what that something was. But there was one thing she was certain of: she wasn't keen on this newcomer. For a start, it was hogging all the attention and Poppy didn't like that at all.

Jack sat beside Evie and gently lifted Buttercup into his arms. Poppy glared at the puppy as Jack fussed and petted her. Meanwhile, Evie looked on, her eyes wide and full of joy.

'She's really soft,' Jack said as he gently handed her back to Evie.

Poppy grunted as she watched Evie bury her face

into the puppy's fur. She felt a growl forming in her throat. Her lips twitched.

*What is going on? Why do we have to have another dog? Am I not enough?*

Then, before she knew it, the growl surfaced, making Mom turn and look. Instantly, Poppy felt bad.

'Sorry,' she whined. 'It just slipped out. Buttercup is cute – honestly.'

She gently licked Mom's hand then cast a sneaky glare back to the puppy.

Buttercup was oblivious to Poppy's mood. Her eyes were fixed on Evie's face. Poppy didn't like this one bit, but fortunately, Jack cheered her up.

'Can we have a game now, Dad?' he asked, pulling on his new T-shirt.

Poppy charged outside, glad to be out of the cottage and away from all that fuss over one little puppy. She raced to the lawn then spun around and barked at Dad and Jack to hurry.

She sped over to Jack and jumped up, but not too high, she didn't want to knock him over. She butted the ball with her nose then barked, 'Come on, kick the ball. Kick the ball!'

Jack did and Poppy galloped after it – well, she intended to gallop.

The ball was just ahead.

She jumped, toppled, then lost her balance. She jumped back up to see Dad dribbling the ball to the other side of the lawn.

Poppy grumbled. *So much for galloping.* Lollop was the word she'd heard her family use. She wanted to be called agile, athletic and graceful.

Dad kicked the ball. She jumped up but it was too high. Jack took possession. Poppy lowered her head, ready to catch the ball this time.

It soared into the air. It went higher and higher then fell back to earth. Poppy was ready. She wagged her tail and barked, 'It's mine!'

She jumped. The ball bounced off her head and rolled across the grass towards Dad.

Jack laughed. 'Oh Poppy!'

'She can't catch anything, can she?' Dad said, laughing.

Poppy stood lapping the slobber from around her jowls. She glared at the ball. Poppy hated being clumsy.

She growled. She howled.

'Come on, Pop,' Dad called.

But Poppy was tired. Her heart was racing and her throat was dry. Right now, all she wanted was a biscuit, or a banana or, even better, an ice cream.

Her ears twitched at the sound of laughter. She looked at Dad and Jack who were tackling each other over the ball, Dad deliberately trying to nudge his son out of the way. However, the laughter wasn't coming from them. Come to think of it, Poppy didn't think it was laughter at all.

The two black and white animals were watching her from the other side of the fence. They stuck their snouts through the gaps in the wire and grunted.

All thoughts of football were replaced with the prospect of making new friends. Poppy trotted over to them, her tail held high and wagging to and fro.

'Hello!' she barked, 'I'm Poppy. And you are?'

'Pigs,' one of them answered.

'Pigs?' Poppy grunted back.

'Pigs.'

'Is that what you're both called?'

'Pigs.'

'OK.' Poppy leaned forward then backed away quickly when her nose nearly touched a snout. 'What shall we play?' she barked.

'Pigs,' they grunted.

'OK…'

Poppy didn't understand this conversation. She jumped and bounced in a circle, barking happily. *So are they both called pigs? I'm not sure what they're trying to tell me, but they want to play. They want to be my friend – and that'll do for me.* She barked and jumped again. She ran a few paces and was overjoyed to see the pigs follow. They ran up and down, Poppy on one side of the fence, the pigs on the other.

As she barked, the pigs continued to grunt, 'Pigs. Pigs. Pigs.'

'Made some new friends there, Poppy?' Dad said.

Dad and Jack walked up to the fence. Jack crouched down as the pigs walked up to him, still grunting loudly.

Poppy looked around. She noticed the treetops peeking up from behind the farm buildings.

*The Wood!* How could she have forgotten?

She thought about the forest back home – the tall grass, rustling leaves, clods of dirt and mud, the squirrels scampering up the trees, the rabbits jumping and playing and the delightful smell of fox, horse, deer, badger and yes, sometimes even dog poo.

Poppy ran across the lawn towards the trees, her body low, ears flapping and jowls pushed back over her teeth. She ran so fast she felt as though she was flying.

# THE WOOD

'Poppy!' Mom whistled. 'Poppy!' she cried out again.

Poppy wanted to investigate the wood more than anything. She was excited just thinking about the squirrels scurrying across the woodland floor and what delicious morsels of food she'd find there. She really didn't want to turn back.

Just then, she heard Dad call out from across the garden.

'She's all right, Jane. Remember what Carol said. The wood is enclosed. Poppy can't go anywhere.'

Hearing this, Poppy ran even faster, until she heard the sound of an engine close by. She saw a large black truck covered in dust stop behind the gate. It had an open-top cab and in the back was…

Poppy's heart skipped a beat.

There was Samson, looking proud and handsome. The sun shone on his black and white fur. He stuck his white chest out and lifted his chin.

Another collie stood beside him. She was a little smaller than Samson. Whereas he sat still with his nose in the air enjoying the sunshine, the other collie paced up and down. She was panting heavily and her eyes darted everywhere. Her fur, which was longer than Samson's, ruffled in the wind. She noticed Poppy and barked loudly.

Samson glared at the other collie, then turned his back on them both.

But the younger collie was undeterred. She barked again.

'Hello! Who are you?'

'Poppy,' said Poppy, happy to meet a potential new friend.

'My name's Bow. I'm training to be a sheepdog.'

'Nice to meet you, Bow,' Poppy barked. Meanwhile, Samson didn't move. All she could see was the back of his head.

Samson and Bow didn't stay for long. Poppy guessed they were going to spend the day working in the field. Meanwhile, seeing as the wood was only yards away, Poppy decided to explore. She turned and, with her nose to the ground, made her way inside.

Once surrounded by trees, she felt the welcoming, cool shade. Tall blades of grass and leaves stroked her face as she pushed her nose into the ground, moving stones and clods of earth aside. She snorted at the smell of rabbit droppings, then quickly ate a few – delicious.

The wildflowers smelt divine, and in the distance she detected the familiar scent of horses. Unlike the forest back home, there were no man-made paths with signs pointing people in various directions: the blue walk, the red walk or the yellow walk, which was the longest route – and her favourite. Here at Buttercup Farm, the paths were narrow and winding. They twisted around the trees and bushes, the earth churned up in places where horses had walked through.

Something moved. Poppy turned quickly to see a squirrel running across the twisting path and into a thicket of tall grass. Her heart raced. The chase was on…

She ploughed through the grass. She jumped around the trees, over the rocks and stones and twisted roots.

Adrenaline coursed through her. The cool woodland air rushed past her face and through her fur.

She barked at the squirrel as it scampered up a tree. She stood looking up at the crisscrossing branches and leaves.

*What would it be like up there? I wonder how many squirrels there are, jumping from branch to branch.*

For a moment, Poppy wished she could climb trees, just like the squirrels. She jumped up, her front paws pressed against the tree trunk. But the branches were too high for her to climb.

Something rustled and snapped behind her. She spun around. She looked left and right.

*Another squirrel maybe? Or perhaps a rabbit?*

She heard the sound of paws padding over dry ground. Running. Grass and bushes rustled, whispering as if to tell her she was not alone. But she knew this already. A wood was never empty. And yet, this was different…

Poppy sniffed the air. Something wasn't right. Suddenly, this wood didn't seem as friendly and exciting a place as she had thought at first. The fur on her back tingled. She sensed something – the problem was she didn't know what that *something* could be.

Pressing her nose against the ground, she walked slowly along the path.

*Perhaps it was a deer?*

Sometimes, though rarely, she saw deer in Childer's Forest, back home. They were very shy and so fast that she didn't get to see them for long. However, one day, she had caught sight of the infamous white stag.

At first, she had been afraid, but her keen senses told her that the stag wasn't a threat. Yet, by the time she'd realised this he'd gone. She hoped to see him again one day.

Poppy's curiosity was mounting. What other creatures and smells were in Buttercup Wood? Poppy ventured farther. It grew darker. Trees clustered closer together, their leaves blocking out the sun and sky.

Then, she heard it again. Rustling. Snapping. A whoosh. The padding of paws.

Poppy lifted her nose and sniffed. The wood was filled with the usual smells she was familiar with: squirrels, grass, flowers, rabbits. But there was something else too.

She sniffed again, then pressed her nose to the floor. Slowly, she walked, sniffing and snorting. That smell was not a woodland animal, she was certain of that.

The excitement and joy she associated with the forest had evaporated some time ago. The comfortable, cool and shady wood suddenly appeared dark and gloomy, threatening and frightening.

*What was that?*

Heavy breaths… and they sounded close by…

That was enough for Poppy. She turned and ran back through the wood, using her keen sense of smell to guide her towards the cottage.

# NEW FRIENDS AND GAMES

Poppy was woken by a strange sound. She lifted her head and twitched her ears. There it was again. It sounded like a croaky scream.

She tilted her head, then heard Dad chuckling.

'It's only the cockerel,' he said, 'telling us it's time to get up.'

Poppy hadn't realised Dad was there. *Have I slept that deeply?* She lay at the top of the stairs, beside the window. It was her favourite spot because from there she could see the farm animals and the wood.

Thoughts of the wood came flooding back. The sound of paw-steps. The feeling of being watched. The unusual scent.

*What was in there?* Poppy stared at the treetops. Now, safely indoors, and with Dad by her side, she didn't feel so afraid.

'Come on,' Dad said, snapping her out of her thoughts. He patted her on the shoulder as he stepped over her. 'Let's get some fresh air while the others are sleeping.'

Poppy followed him outside.

It was still early. The air was a little cool, the grass damp and the sky turning to muted shades of pinks, blues and yellows. Birds flew from treetop to treetop and the pigs grunted softly into the ground.

A farmer was working in the field across from the cottage. His whistles pierced the stillness as he instructed his collie to herd the sheep.

Poppy sniffed the grass, recognising the scents of various animals that had been out during the night.

Jack's football was still there, sitting in the middle of the lawn.

As if reading her mind, Dad kicked the ball towards her. Poppy barked. 'I'll catch it this time!'

And she did.

She lifted her head, the ball firmly held between her jaws, and trotted away. Her head swayed from side to side, just like her tail.

She was so proud! *Look at me*, she wanted to say, but didn't dare in case she dropped the ball.

Dad laughed. He ran up to her but Poppy quickly changed direction and gained speed. She glanced over her shoulder and was thrilled to see him following.

Eventually, he caught up. He grinned as he held the ball and tried pulling it out of her grasp. Poppy loved playing tug-of-war. She growled happily and pulled back.

Finally, she decided to let go. Just this once.

'Ready?' Dad said, then kicked the ball high into the air.

Poppy's eyes were fixed on the ball. As it came back down, she launched herself up. She hoped Samson was nearby to see this. She stretched her neck and reached… reached…

The ball whistled past her.

She looked over her shoulder to see the ball bouncing across the lawn.

Poppy raced after it. *Stupid ball.*

But Dad beat her to it. Poppy ran beside him, jumping and barking.

Each time she lunged, Dad was quicker. He sidestepped past. He turned and ran with the ball, dribbling it up and down the lawn.

'All right, all right,' Dad said, with laughter in his voice. He stopped, holding the ball in his hands, and smiled at her. 'Ready?'

He kicked the ball towards her. Poppy lunged, mouth open, ready to take it. But she butted it with her nose instead, sending the ball shooting off in the opposite direction.

Dad caught it and threw the ball again. Poppy nose-butted it back, her jowls slapping together and slobber splattering across her muzzle.

Poppy grumbled. Why couldn't she catch the ball? She had done it the first time.

She wished she was quicker, sharper and lighter. She wished she was more like the collie in the field across the road. Then she recognised who it was – Samson.

Poppy sat and watched the collie at work. Dad and the football were now forgotten. The field opposite was on a slight incline and from where she sat, she had the perfect view. She watched Samson run around the sheep in response to Colin's whistles. She had no idea what the whistles meant, but it was clear that Samson did.

To each whistle, he responded without hesitation and the sheep responded to him too. He had complete control. He circled the sheep. He stopped. Lay down. Stood up. Poppy was impressed by his focus, concentration and skill. She wished she could be more like him.

The pigs were grunting at her. As much as she loved watching Samson work, it was making her feel useless. While he controlled a flock of sheep, she struggled to catch a football. So she decided to say hello to the pigs instead.

'Good morning!' she howled.

'Pigs. Pigs,' they replied.

She stopped at the gate and gently leaned her nose against the wire. The pigs stepped forward, grunting and pushing their snouts towards her.

One of the pigs touched her nose. Poppy jumped back.

'Steady, there,' she growled again.

Dad appeared beside her. He placed his hand on the back of her head and gently stroked her ears. She heard him chuckle.

The pigs grunted louder. Poppy guessed they were greeting Dad too. She couldn't help but feel confused though. She could communicate with most animals – elephants, zebras, cats, even lions. But the pigs at Buttercup Farm were a mystery. Yet, she could sense they were just as keen to be friends as she was.

Poppy trotted up and down the fence and was thrilled to see the pigs follow her, grunting as they came. When she turned around, she noticed Dad watching them as well. She ran faster. The pigs followed.

'Can you say anything else?' she barked, happily.

'Pigs.'

'How about my name? Can you say Poppy?'

'Pigs.'

'No. Poppy.' She slowed down a little, seeing the pigs nudging each other as they tried to keep up. They grunted loudly. Dad was laughing.

'Poppy,' she barked. 'Say Poppy.'

'Pigs.'

She stopped and looked at them. The pigs stood side by side, gazing up at her. Their grunts died down into soft moans. They pushed their snouts through the fence again. Poppy wagged her tail and gently brushed her nose against theirs.

OK, so they didn't speak the same language, but that didn't matter because they were now friends. *Maybe they choose not to communicate that way?* There were, Poppy realised, many other ways to converse. Body language. Play. Expression. Play. Mannerisms. Play!

She looked up, wondering which other animals she could befriend, then stumbled backwards seeing the cockerel walking towards her.

He was a striking bird. His deep green, russet and gold plumage shone in the sun. He approached without any caution – considering she was so much bigger than him.

Fortunately, her encounter with the pigs had bolstered her confidence a little, and so she stepped forward and growled, 'Good morning, I'm Poppy.'

The cockerel paused. He watched her and then threw his head back and called, 'Cock-a-doodle-doo!' At the 'doo', his voice croaked and wobbled.

Poppy turned and ran. She did the first thing she always did when she was afraid. She went to Dad.

He crouched down and opened his arms. The moment she reached him, he folded them around her.

'Did he frighten you?' he said softly against her ear. 'Don't worry, Pops. He won't hurt you.' Dad looked into her face.

Poppy leaned forward and licked his nose. She heard the click of a window opening.

'Dad, breakfast's ready!' Evie called.

Dad stood up but Poppy was already running back to the cottage. She'd heard one of her favourite words – Breakfast!

# NEW NEIGHBOURS

Poppy followed Dad and Jack into the garden. She licked her lips, still tasting the delicious sausages and eggs. She loved holidays. She was always treated to the food she'd never have at home. Breakfast was usually a dental stick, but not this week. And there were six more mornings ahead to enjoy a bowl of delicious eggs and sausages.

While Jack practised his football skills, Dad stood at the gate talking to someone. Poppy decided to go and investigate. She trotted down the gravel drive. As she approached, she heard Dad say, 'the cockerel scared her a bit.'

Poppy sat beside Dad and looked up at the farmer, Colin Briggs, who was leaning against the gate.

He smiled at Poppy.

'The animals are used to dogs and people, so there's nothing to worry about. Olde Red was probably just saying hello.'

Dad gently stroked Poppy's ear. This felt nice, so Poppy leaned against him – relishing the fuss. The humans continued to talk, but Poppy was no longer listening. She was distracted by Samson, who'd walked up to Colin and now sat behind him. She couldn't tear her eyes off the collie.

She wanted to greet him. To say hello as she had done with the pigs and Olde Red, but she was afraid. Afraid of what reaction she would get. Yet, she was determined to say something. She took a deep breath. She was about to give a polite and friendly growl, when Samson turned away.

He leapt on to the back of the truck, making the feat look easy. Poppy knew if she tried doing that, she'd be scrambling on to the truck with her front paws while her back legs frantically trod thin air.

She gazed at the handsome hound. He looked proud and distinguished, his nose twitching and face tilted against the morning sun. Then, to her surprise, he glanced her way. Their eyes met. She barked, before losing her nerve.

'Good morning, Samson.'

The big collie turned away again and Poppy's heart sank.

*He's probably still annoyed with me for running into him at the beach.*

'I wouldn't bother with Samson,' Colin said to Poppy. 'He's not the friendliest. You'd get more joy from Carol's two, Oliver and Olive.'

Poppy looked towards the farmhouse. The two dogs were laid out on their fluffy beds. Olive was lying on her stomach while Oliver sprawled out on his back, legs pointing up to the sky.

The farmer smiled at Poppy. 'You'll have more fun with those two, believe me,' he said.

Poppy doubted it, her ears twitching against the sound of their grunts and snores.

Colin whistled, and suddenly Bow, the younger collie, appeared at his side. Unlike Samson, she greeted Dad and Poppy with a friendly bark.

'This is Bow,' Colin said as he made a fuss of her. 'She's only a year old. I'm training her at the moment out on the field with Samson.'

'She's a beauty,' Dad said.

Hearing this, Poppy turned and pressed her cheek against Dad's leg.

'She's a looker like our Pops,' he said, then laid his hand on the top of Poppy's head.

Poppy smiled proudly.

'Off you go, girl,' Colin said. Bow turned and leapt into the truck. She looked up at Samson and whined softly – but the big collie ignored her too.

Poppy read the disappointment on Bow's face and she couldn't help feeling sorry for her.

But just then, she had the strangest feeling… She was being watched.

Poppy's ears twitched. She felt the fur rise along her back. She looked around. Carol was feeding the pigs. The goat was standing with its eyes closed enjoying a spot of sunbathing. Poppy was pleased to see that Olde Red was nowhere in sight, and the hens were pecking at the ground, clucking softly as they went about their business. Olive and Oliver were still sleeping.

*So who is watching me?*

Mom and Evie were still in the cottage and Jack was now kicking his football against the barn.

Poppy's ears twitched. She turned to Dad, Colin, Bow and then Samson. No one seemed alarmed. She lifted her chin and sniffed. She definitely detected something – but what it was, she couldn't say.

SNAP. CRUNCH. RUSTLE. *Was it leaves, grass, brambles or bushes?*

Poppy turned towards the wood. The smell was stronger in that direction. There was nothing else for it. She had to investigate.

# THE BEST SMELL IN THE WORLD

Dad and Colin's voices carried around the farmyard, the cottage's garden and towards the wood where Poppy was cautiously heading.

Her heartbeat raced as she took one slow step at a time. Her blood pounded against her ears. Her heart hammered against her chest.

The trees stood tall and still. Birds rustled the leaves as they settled on the branches. Sunlight filtered through the canopy of leaves. Cool and shady, it looked so inviting on such a hot morning.

There was hardly a breeze to disturb the long grass. Everything looked serene, at peace, empty. But

Poppy knew better. Inside the wood there were families. Families of mice, foxes, badgers, rabbits, squirrels, birds and more creatures that Poppy couldn't even think of. It was home for many and enjoyed by them all. However, the smell she was detecting was not a familiar forest smell.

Poppy's hackles rose. She was nervous. But despite this, she continued making her way, step by step, into the wood.

Poppy jumped as two rabbits shot out from beneath a hedge and raced into the trees. Their white tails bobbed up and down as they ran down the twisting, uneven path, jumping over roots and then charging into a mass of bracken.

It had happened so fast. One minute she was alone, the next there were two rabbits, and now she was alone once again. She stared at the bracken, the leaves still swaying where they'd dived for cover. Her nose twitched. The smell of rabbit was rich in the air. She wondered if it had been the rabbits she'd heard earlier. Her ears quivered at the sound of small paws scampering through bracken and brambles.

She took a deep sniff, breathing in the smell of rabbit. The urge to chase them was irresistible.

She charged through the bracken. She jumped over thick, twisted roots. The scent was still strong. She had to be close.

'Where are you?' she barked. 'Come on, show yourself. I only want to play.'

Poppy pressed her nose into the woodland floor then snorted. *Oh my word, that smell!*

In an instant, she'd forgotten all about the rabbits. She took a deep, deep breath. That smell was divine, one of her favourite fragrances in the whole world.

She rubbed her head along the floor, then her shoulder. She groaned with pleasure, rolling on to her back and wriggling into the ground, covering herself with the smell.

'Poppy!'

Poppy stopped. She recognised Dad's voice, then heard his whistle, sharp and loud.

'Poppy, where are you?'

She rolled on to her stomach and looked around.

'Poppy!'

That was Mom calling, so she knew she couldn't waste any more time. Reluctantly, she left the beautifully smelly spot and ran back through the wood, using the sound of her pawrents' voices to guide her.

As she ran, the smell drifted under her nose. She smelt wonderful. Hopefully, Samson was still at the farm. If there was one thing guaranteed to catch a dog's attention it was smells – and she smelt fabulous!

# WASH AND BLOW-DRY

Poppy raced out of the wood to see Mom standing on the driveway looking for her. She was disappointed to find Colin's truck had gone, and with it his two collies.

*Never mind. I'm sure I'll still smell lovely by the time Samson returns.*

She stopped running the minute she noticed the look on Mom's face. Mom's expression changed from relief to shock, then… what was that? Anger? Sadness? Disgust?

*What's happened?*

Mom's eyes opened wide. She slowly shook her head then, when Poppy stopped in front of her, she scrunched up her face and cried, 'Jon! Jon!'

Poppy looked over her shoulder. *Whatever's the matter?* Dad walked out of the cottage.

'What is it?' he said, then seeing Poppy, 'Ah, you've found her. Come on then, let's get going.'

'Er, not yet,' Mom said.

Dad stood beside Mom. They both stared at Poppy.

'What on earth…,?' Dad's voice trailed away. He took a deep breath and Poppy noticed him scrunch his face too.

'It's all matted in her fur… just look! And the smell…' Mom held her hand over her nose and mouth. 'Oh Poppy, that's disgusting.'

'You know what that is, don't you?' Dad said. Then, before Mom could answer, 'That's fox poo.'

Mom turned around and marched over to the barn. There was a tap in the wall with a hosepipe connected to it. It dawned on Poppy what was going to happen next. She started backing away, but Dad stepped forward and seized her by the collar.

'No you don't,' he said, stopping her in her tracks.

Mom walked towards her, holding the long, yellow snake-like hose.

Poppy whined. 'No. Not water!' She tugged and pulled but Dad held on tightly. 'But the smell!' she barked. 'Don't get rid of the beautiful smell!'

Mom turned the hose on and a jet of cold water covered Poppy from head to tail. While Mom soaked her, holding on tightly to her collar, Dad fetched a bottle out of the cottage. Her pawrents called it shampoo and they said the smell was vanilla. Whatever it was, Poppy didn't like it. Dad coated her in this shampoo, roughly massaging it into her fur, covering her in white foam.

Poppy scowled and grumbled. Her mood was made worse when she heard snorting – or was it burping? No. It was laughter, definitely laughter. Throaty, nasal chuckles came from the farmhouse.

Poppy sighed then looked past Dad to see Oliver and Olive. They stared at her through the fence. They were loving every minute.

*I wouldn't be surprised if they enjoyed being bathed,* Poppy thought, glaring at them. *I can just see them at the dog parlour, being fussed and preened.* Poppy couldn't think of anything worse. She wasn't a fan of the groomers. She hated the water, and even worse, those hairdryers!

She groaned and grumbled, hearing Oliver still laughing. His loud snorts carried around the farmyard. His body shuddered as he snorted again and again before sneezing loudly and covering Olive in something frothy.

Poppy smiled. She looked back towards the wood, certain that she'd be able to find the spot again and re-cover herself in that scent before Samson returned. But just then, a cold jet of water splashed her face and she concluded that if this is what happened whenever she smelt so nice, then perhaps it was better if she didn't bother.

Tall grass swayed in the breeze – only, Poppy realised, there was no breeze. She narrowed her eyes and peered at the spot between the trees, to a cluster of grass, nettles and ferns. Something moved. Was it another rabbit? She wished she could find out, but Dad still had hold of her while Mom washed away the disgustingly sweet-smelling shampoo.

Something orange – or was it brown? – appeared amidst the undergrowth.

It moved slowly, and then the sunlight caught something that glinted in the light. Poppy gulped. It was a pair of eyes.

Poppy was too afraid to move. She stared at the eyes that stared right back from amongst the grass and ferns. This reminded her of something…

She cast her mind back to when she was at the safari park. She felt the fear, panic and dread wash over her as she thought of that moment when, from out of the tall grass, something stared at her. Remembering those eyes made her tremble. It had been a wolf – and she'd narrowly got away with her life.

Did that mean that here, now, in the small wood at Buttercup Farm, a wolf was lurking, waiting to attack? It would certainly explain the unusual smell. But no. Poppy knew all too well what a wolf looked and smelt like. What she detected here in Buttercup Wood was something different. This wasn't a wolf, nor was it a fox. So, what could it be?

She thought back to Jack's vast collection of books and DVDs on animals. Then she remembered what Jack had said about the new addition to the safari park…

It was the night before their holiday. Bags were packed and stacked up in the hallway.

Mom returned from the chippy carrying a big bag of food.

Poppy jumped up on the settee and settled in between Jack and Evie. She watched the cartons of food being handed out. Battered sausage. Cod. Chips. Curry Sauce. Mushy peas. It all smelt delicious.

Poppy edged closer to Evie. She was usually the soft touch so Poppy knew she'd at least win a chip.

Meanwhile, Jack poised his new safari park book on his lap whilst balancing his tray of sausage and chips.

'Can we go to the zoo on holiday?' he asked.

'Of course,' Mom said, shaking vinegar on to her chips.

Evie wriggled and shook her feet. 'I'm so excited!' she said, 'I won't be able to sleep tonight.'

'I wonder if they've got dholes,' Jack said.

Poppy turned away from Evie's tray of food and peered over Jack's shoulder. She thought she knew all the animals in Jack's book, but this was the first time she'd heard him mention a dhole.

'A what?' Dad said.

'A dhole. It's a new animal at the safari park. It says here that they come from Asia.'

Poppy looked at the pictures. The dhole looked like a reddish-brown dog or fox with pointy ears, a long narrow face and a black bushy tail.

*I wonder if they're dangerous.*

Then, as if reading her mind, Jack said, 'They're like wolves in that they don't bark and they hunt in packs… Their favourite food is deer.'

Poppy shivered, thinking of the young deer that roamed Childer's Forest.

'It says,' Jack continued, 'that they're also known as whistling dogs or the Indian wild dog.'

Poppy shuddered, remembering those African wild dogs and the wolves at the safari park. She hoped never to meet one again.

Poppy trembled and whined at the memory. And now, there was a dhole – a whistling dog, an Indian wild dog – lurking in Buttercup Wood.

Finally, Mom turned the hose off. Poppy sighed. *And about time too.*

Poppy looked away from the wood, trying to put thoughts of a savage wild dog to the back of her mind. She saw Mom walk back inside while Dad rolled the hose back up into its reel.

She shook herself, feeling the water lift from her coat and spray Dad.

'Thanks for that, Poppy,' he said, then laughed. 'Come on, let's get you inside.'

Poppy trotted after him, glad to be further away from the wood.

Jack and Evie were standing in the hallway. Poppy glared at the sight of Buttercup all safe and dry in Evie's arms. She caught the expression on the puppy's face and thought how smug it looked.

*If Buttercup went into the wood then I'm sure she'd roll in that smell too. What dog wouldn't? Then we'd see who was smiling…*

She was so busy glaring at Buttercup that she didn't realise what was coming until it was too late.

First, an awful noise sent Poppy jumping back in fright. Her eyes nearly popped out of their sockets. She growl-howled.

'What's that? I don't like it. Turn it off!'

But the deafening noise continued. It rattled. It roared.

Then she felt it. Warm, fast air, blasting her fur. Poppy scrunched her eyes shut. *Not the hairdryer!*

But she couldn't move. She was trapped. Mom crouched down to Poppy's level. Jack and Evie stood behind her, blocking her escape.

'Come on, now,' Mom said, softly. She turned the speed of the hairdryer down and the roaring sound quietened a little. It was much softer and gentler. In fact, Poppy realised, it was a bit more bearable.

'The sooner we get you dry, the sooner we can get going,' Mom said.

'Can we have ice cream when we get there?' Evie asked.

Poppy's ears twitched. *Ice cream?*

'Absolutely,' Mom replied. 'What flavour?'

'I'll have cookies and cream, please,' Jack said.

'Strawberry, please,' Evie said, then licked her lips. 'Can I have sprinkles on it too?'

Mom laughed. 'Of course.'

'Well, as we're on holiday,' Dad said, walking over and gently rubbing the damp fur on Poppy's back, 'I think we should treat Poppy to one too.'

Poppy barked. 'Yes! Strawberry for me too, please.'

'That's settled then,' Mom said. 'As soon as Poppy's dry, we'll head off to Brixham and get those ice creams.'

Poppy threw her head back and howled.

'Brixham! I love Brixham. They have the best ice cream parlours!' Poppy jumped around and howled once more. 'Hurry up and get me dry!'

# A MYSTERIOUS FIGURE IN THE WOOD

Poppy was on Neighbourhood Watch duty. She sat at the top of the stairs and looked out of the window, while the rest of the family gathered their things: bags, football, bucket, spade, towels…she could guess where they were going. The beach.

She was happy. The sun was shining. It was another glorious summer's day and what better way to spend the day than at the beach – just so long as no one decided to go into the sea.

Whilst her family rushed around, Jack and Evie giggling excitedly about the day ahead, Poppy stared at the wood. She glared at the treetops. She squinted at the tree trunks and the shady darkness within.

*What was in there? Could it be a dhole, a whistling dog, an Indian Wild Dog?*

Poppy grunted. There was a peculiar scent around that wood and she was itching to find out what it was. An exotic creature from India would certainly explain it. She twitched her ears, listening out for an unusual bark, howl or whistle.

There was nothing. Nothing out of place. Nothing to disturb the stillness of the Devonshire countryside.

Suddenly, Olde Red called out. Poppy jumped. She couldn't get used to his croaky cock-a-doodle-doo. Mom laughed every time. She said it sounded as if he was being strangled.

Poppy watched Olde Red strut around the pond, his sharp eyes watching the ducks as they swam happily. The ducks were soaking up the sun, not a bit bothered by the big, colourful rooster.

Meanwhile, the geese waddled past him, honking to each other as they went. *They don't seem scared of anything*, Poppy thought, realising that the geese made her just as uneasy as Olde Red.

The front door to the farmhouse was ajar. The patio was flooded with sunlight and there, laid out on their beds, were Oliver and Olive.

Samson was nowhere to be seen. Poppy guessed he was working with Colin.

Carol stepped outside and sat on the doorstep. Oliver and Olive rolled off their beds and pressed their noses into her lap, their short tails wagging. They

64

lapped up the food she gave them. Poppy licked her lips, wondering what tasty morsels they were devouring. Lucky pups.

'Poppy! Come on!'

Poppy spun around only to realise her family were waiting for her. Her shift of Neighbourhood Watch was over. She raced downstairs and outside. Mom was already in the car with Evie. Meanwhile, Jack was engrossed in kicking his football high into the air.

Dad followed Poppy outside and locked the door behind him. As Poppy waited, she looked at the wood. She growled softly and narrowed her eyes, taking in every detail – every shadow and every plant.

A squirrel scampered up a tree. Two pigeons flew out from a treetop and landed on a telephone wire.

Poppy's ears twitched. Her keen sense of hearing had detected movement within the undergrowth. The paw-steps were heavier than those of a rabbit, mouse or bird.

'Are you a dhole?' she growled, glaring into the wood. 'If you are, then how did you get here?'

'Come on,' Dad said, tapping the top of her head lightly.

Poppy glanced at him then turned to follow – but just then…

*What was that, between the branches of that bush? Something moved…*

A light colour flashed against the darker shades of the wood. A reddish-brown appeared against the forest's eerie shadows. *It's got to be a fox,* Poppy thought. Yet, there was something about it. Something not quite right. She'd seen foxes many times. She'd heard them and smelt them. The figure may have moved fast, but she'd seen enough to realise it didn't move like a fox. So that could only mean one thing – it had to be a dhole.

Poppy barked. Her heart raced. She gulped. Her throat suddenly felt tight and she became breathless. A pair of eyes were staring at her.

Poppy had seen enough. With one more bark, she turned tail and ran into the car.

Soon they were out on the coastal road, with fields on one side and the open sea on the other. Poppy pushed thoughts about the mysterious figure in the wood to the back of her mind.

She watched enviously as Evie held Buttercup up to the window. The puppy pressed her nose against the glass.

'Look, Buttercup. We're nearly there.' Evie giggled, then looked at Poppy.

Poppy leaned forward and kissed Evie's cheek. 'I'm here too, you know,' she whined.

Evie giggled again and returned Poppy's kiss, planting her lips firmly on her cheek.

Meanwhile, Buttercup was too immersed in the scenery whizzing passed to notice Poppy.

*Typical,* Poppy thought. *What do I have to do to get Buttercup's attention?*

'Shall we build a big sandcastle first, Jack?' Evie said.

Her brother agreed, on one condition. 'As long as we play football with Dad afterwards,' he said.

'OK. And then we'll go in the sea.'

Both agreed to this perfect plan, but Poppy wasn't so thrilled. She looked at Buttercup, wondering what her thoughts were on the matter.

Evie held the puppy up to her face. 'You'll love the beach,' she said, her cheeks flushed and her eyes bright. 'We'll collect shells to put on the sandcastle. Then we'll look for crabs and fish in the rock pools. Then we'll go into the sea and jump over the waves. I'm going to go up to my knees today.'

Buttercup gazed up into Evie's face. Poppy growled quietly.

'Don't go out too far, Evie!' Poppy whined. 'Why don't we stay on the sand? Buttercup wouldn't like the sea, believe me.' She snuffled into Buttercup's soft ears. 'Stick to dry land.'

Mom turned in her seat and looked at them. 'Is Poppy talking to Buttercup?'

Evie kissed the puppy's ears. 'And Buttercup loves Poppy too – look.' She lifted her towards Poppy until pup and Pop touched noses.

Dad glanced at them in the rear-view mirror. 'So, Poppy and Buttercup are best friends.' Poppy heard the chuckle in his voice. Something amused him – but she couldn't think what it could be.

Poppy pressed on.

'Buttercup,' she barked, 'the sea is wet and salty. It tastes horrid and your fur will get matted. And don't get me started on the seaweed…'

Jack was laughing. He leaned over and hugged Poppy.

'You see, Buttercup? They know I'm right!' she howled.

'Pop,' Dad said, smiling, 'you liked the hairdryer once you gave it a try. If you just give the sea a chance, you'd like that too.'

Poppy stared at the back of Dad's head.

'Dad, I love you, but sometimes you say the silliest things,' she growled.

# FUN AND SUNSHINE

It was the best sandcastle Poppy had ever seen. Jack and Evie had excelled themselves this time.

Poppy lay beside it, proud of the Robinsons' creation. Jack and Evie had dug a moat around the castle and filled it with seawater. Mom helped decorate the castle with seashells. Dad had even gone to the beach shop and bought flags to stick in the towers.

In Poppy's opinion, it was the best one on the beach. She crossed her paws, lifted her face to the sun and grunted with pride.

'OK, then,' Mom said as she rummaged in her beach bag. Poppy heard her muttering to herself, 'Where is it now? Where did I put it?'

Poppy knew what was coming, so she sat up and waited.

Mom turned around, holding her camera aloft like a trophy. Her face lit up seeing Poppy already posing beside the castle.

'I swear Poppy can read minds!' she said as everyone else groaned at the sight of the camera.

'Oh, come on!' Mom said brightly. She knelt on the towel while Dad crouched behind Jack, Evie and Poppy.

The instant Mom had taken not one photo, not two, but three, Jack scooped up his football. Dad and Evie followed, leaving Mom and Buttercup to sunbathe.

Poppy ran after them. She loved the feel of the soft grains of sand between her pads. She spun around, barking excitedly.

While Dad, Jack and Evie played a game of piggy-in-the-middle, Poppy decided to try and dig to the bottom of this massive sandpit. She'd managed it at home, so why not here? So she dug, and dug. And dug.

Sand flew out behind her. Her tail swished and her front legs pummelled into the sand until, eventually, she grew tired. Her legs ached and she needed a drink.

As though he'd read her mind, Jack appeared with a bottle of water. He tipped it up and Poppy lapped the cold, refreshing liquid. Not one drop escaped her lips.

Poppy thanked Jack by licking his hand, then she stood up wagging her tail and waited for the next game.

Evie looked up at Dad and grinned, squinting against the sun.

'Dad, can we go into the sea now?'

Poppy grunted. *Why?*

Evie looked at Poppy and her grin deepened. 'Let's try getting Poppy in there too.'

Jack agreed, but Poppy backed away and growl-howled, 'I'll be all right here with Mom and Buttercup.'

Dad stepped forward, holding his arms out to her.

'Come on, you,' he said. 'Honestly, you'll love it if you just give it a try. Remember the hairdryer? You enjoyed that in the end.'

Poppy groaned. 'I wish you'd stop going on about that hairdryer,' she grunted. 'And besides, I don't agree. I will never – ever – like the sea.'

Dad smiled. 'Look at the others…'

Poppy followed his gaze and watched dogs barking, jumping and running through the water. She had to admit, they all looked happy. But she was happy right where she was. She didn't need the water to have fun.

Suddenly, and without warning, Dad scooped her up in his arms.

'Nooo!' Poppy howled, closing her eyes.

'Oh, Poppy!' she heard Mom say, but there was laughter in her voice. Mom was scrambling about. Poppy looked up, her ears flapping over her face and her jowls swinging as Dad jogged across the sand.

'Great,' she grumbled. 'Mom's taking another photo.'

Dad carried her into the sea while Jack and Evie ran beside them. Poppy noticed people stop and stare. Some were laughing. Some dogs were laughing too.

*Oh, the indignity of it.*

But Poppy knew what she was going to do the minute Dad let go.

She braced herself. Dad waded into the sea up to his knees, then he gently lowered Poppy into the water. The waves lapped over her, soaking her fur. She felt the force of the water pushing backwards and forwards, making her stumble. Then, feeling Dad's hands release her, she ran.

Poppy leapt over the waves. She was determined to reach dry land as fast as she could. She dodged past people and swerved around dogs.

Seagulls called out from above, the water splish-splashed as she ploughed through the waves. Poppy tasted and smelt salt on her tongue as the water splashed over her nose. Yet, she also felt the fresh sea breeze against her face, lifting her jowls. She felt the warm sun on her back, already drying her fur.

Once back on the sand, Poppy caught sight of Mom and Buttercup – both were laid out enjoying the sun. She sprinted towards them.

The moment Mom saw Poppy, she sat up and grabbed her camera. She took shot after shot – capturing Poppy as she charged. As Poppy drew nearer, though, Mom's smile faltered. Poppy wasn't slowing down.

In no time she was on the towel, jumping all over her, growling, barking and shaking water and wet sand all over the place.

'Poppy!' Mom cried. She closed her eyes and looked away while Poppy shook herself again.

When she finally stopped to catch her breath, she noticed Buttercup was watching her. The retriever had that same fixed smile on her face. *Then again,* Poppy thought, *she would have, wouldn't she? Buttercup doesn't have to go into that horrible sea. Instead, she's able to sit with Mom and sunbathe and watch me make a fool of myself.*

Poppy barked, 'It's not fair. Why should I go in the water and not Buttercup?' She jumped around the little dog then lunged at her after every few steps, trying to get a reaction out of her. To be honest, Poppy realised, a reaction from Buttercup would have been nice. Someone to wrestle with, run with, play with…

Mom picked Buttercup up and handed her to Evie who had followed Poppy out of the sea.

'Poppy, calm down,' Mom said softly. She knelt up and held her by the collar. She smiled into Poppy's eyes as she stroked her ears and made soft shushing sounds.

Slowly, Poppy's heartbeat settled to its usual, gentle rhythm. She sneezed, the salt and sand tickling her nose.

'There, there,' Mom cooed.

Poppy's breathing slowed down and she settled beside Mom. Dad leaned over and ruffled the top of her head. He wasn't cross, he was laughing.

'Do you think Poppy would go in if Buttercup joined her?' Dad laughed.

'She was probably telling Buttercup to come with her,' Jack said, giggling.

'Buttercup isn't getting wet,' Evie said, hugging the puppy against her chest.

'I wonder…' Mom's voice trailed away. 'Poppy was probably thinking if she had to go in, then why shouldn't Buttercup.'

Poppy looked from one to the other. She nudged Mom's arm with her wet nose.

'Thank you, Mom,' she groaned then licked her arm. 'And I'm sorry I covered you in wet sand.'

Poppy concluded that despite the fact that she'd been pleasantly surprised by how nice the hairdryer was, the sea was not the same thing. For a start, the hairdryer may be noisy, but the heat felt nice against her fur, the warm air blowing her coat and tickling her skin – it was relaxing. But the sea, well that was completely different.

For one thing, the water was cold; secondly, she hated getting wet; and finally, why couldn't it keep still? What was with those waves? Rising and falling, rolling backwards and forwards. It made her head feel so funny that she thought she'd fall over. There was no end to it either, the water just went on and on and on…

# ICE CREAM MAKES EVERYTHING BETTER

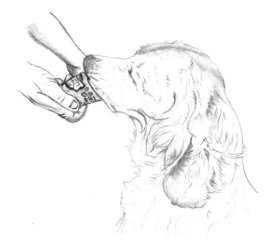

A faint scent carried in the air. As it grew stronger it tickled Poppy's nose, rousing her sensitive sense of smell. It was a familiar smell and one that made all thoughts of the sea disappear. Ice cream!

Poppy followed the scent and saw that there was an ice cream van parked on the beach.

Jumping to her feet, she looked up at Dad and barked, 'Ice cream, there's ice cream!'

She trotted beside Dad, Jack and Evie. She looked from the van to Dad and back to the van again, barking excitedly as she went along. She was skipping. Tail swinging. Thoughts of Buttercup and the rolling sea were now pushed to the farthest regions of her mind.

*Ice cream. Glorious ice cream. Cool, soft and creamy ice cream.*

Poppy's stomach rumbled.

While Jack and Evie decided what to have, Poppy noticed that the queue was getting smaller. By the time they reached the van, the last person was leaving, their hands full of yummy wafer cornets filled with soft, swirly ice cream.

Poppy resisted the urge to leap up and snap the delicious treats out of their hands. Instead, she noted the friendly expression on the ice cream man's face. He leaned out of the window and smiled at Poppy. She didn't need any encouragement. Just as he said, 'Hello,' Poppy jumped up at the counter and whined, groaning and howling in greeting.

The man laughed. 'And what would you like, cutie?'

'Strawberry ice cream… please,' Poppy howled. Her tail wagged so much it made her bottom swish.

Dad stood next to her and pulled his wallet from the back pocket of his shorts.

'Two double-scoop vanilla cornets and two screwballs please,' he said and then looked at Poppy.

She stood with her paws on the counter, peering at the pictures on the window of ice cream, ice lollies and slushies.

'Strawberry please,' she whined then looked up at Dad, feeling the long strings of drool swinging from her jowls.

'And a strawberry doggo ice cream please,' Dad said.

Poppy barked and barked again, giving the man her brightest goldie smile. It didn't go unnoticed, either, that Dad had only ordered one doggie ice cream.

*But what about Buttercup? Does this mean I have to share?*

When the man handed the delights to Dad, Poppy couldn't contain her excitement – not that she'd been doing a good job of controlling it anyway. At the sight of the irresistible treats, she finally ran out of patience.

She leapt up at Dad, barking and grunting as they walked back to Mom and Buttercup.

'Gimme, gimme!'

'Wait. Just wait,' Dad said, then licked the tip of his ice cream.

Mom took her cornet from Dad. A family nearby sat laughing at Poppy. She loved making people laugh, so this fuelled her excitement and impatience further.

Dad peeled off the foil top and held the white tub out for her. Speckles of ice glistened on the surface of the pink ice cream, almost calling to her. *Eat me…*

Poppy dived. She lapped. She slurped. She gobbled the ice cream down hungrily. When she'd licked the tub clean, she bit into the side, holding it by the rim hoping to salvage a little bit more. Dad tried prising it out of her mouth.

'Leave it,' he said and Poppy instantly let go.

She looked up at him and licked her nose. She snorted loudly then heard people laughing. As she looked around she noticed a family watching her. Seeing she was entertaining folk made her feel even happier until she realised something… she hadn't saved any ice cream for Buttercup! Did this mean she was in trouble?

Mom leaned over with a baby wipe. 'Oh Poppy, you've got ice cream all over your face.' Mom's smile told Poppy that she wasn't in trouble after all. Maybe Buttercup was too young to enjoy ice cream. Mom wiped Poppy's face and ears with the scented, moist cloth. Poppy tried moving her head away but Mom wouldn't let her. She was intent on getting Poppy clean.

Just as Mom finished, Dad took a bite from his wafer cone. The sound of crunching caught Poppy's attention. She lifted her paw to Dad and looked at him with pleading eyes. The smile on his face told her that she'd succeeded. She grinned as he lowered the cornet down to her.

'Now, gently,' he said.

Poppy remembered her manners and gently took the cone from him. The cornet covered her snout like a long, golden pointed nose.

This not only made her family laugh but others nearby too.

Poppy loved this. She never tired of making people laugh, it gave her the best feeling in the world. But then something caught her eye that made her pause.

Samson was on the beach. And he was looking at her.

Poppy's smile faded. She stood very still, wishing the sand would open up and swallow her.

There was nowhere to hide, all she could do was stand there, with the cornet over her nose, while Samson looked on.

Of all the dogs to witness her craziness, it had to be him. She suppressed a whimper at the sight of his disapproving face.

He lifted his chin. She could imagine what he was thinking: *Stupid dog, she looks ridiculous.*

Meanwhile, Flo stood beside Samson, and unlike her handsome collie, she was laughing. She said his name and they ran across the beach together – but not before Samson gave Poppy one last stern look.

She watched him running beside Flo.

She wondered how long he'd been watching her. *Did he see me covered in ice cream?* She groaned and dropped the cornet. She wondered if he'd seen Mom mopping her face with the baby wipe or – even worse – Dad carrying her into the sea.

Poppy quickly ate the cornet then lay down beside Mom with a grunt. She crossed her paws, lifted her head and pushed her shoulders back, hoping to regain her dignity and appear more like a pedigree Woodville Retriever than a clown.

Her nose twitched. She smelt food. Then she noticed Dad and Jack walking towards them. Funny, she hadn't noticed they'd left. More importantly, she noticed what Jack was holding. A hotdog!

When Jack sat down, Poppy tried sitting on his lap. Her nose was inches away from his face.

'Can I have some, please? Sharing is caring,' she whined, forgetting all about Samson and the sea.

She glanced across to Buttercup. Surprisingly, the little one didn't seem disappointed by not having an ice cream.

*That's just as well*, Poppy thought. *If she's too young for ice cream, then she definitely wouldn't be allowed a hot dog.*

This pleased Poppy, yet she felt sorry for the little one. Maybe she should try harder to make friends with Buttercup – but that didn't mean sharing her food. No, Poppy drew the line there.

# AT THE END OF THE DAY

Poppy followed Dad outside. While Mom was getting Jack and Evie ready for bed, he sat out on the patio drinking his coffee. He sighed deeply and looked up at the sky.

The sun was setting and flooding the sky with deep golds and oranges. The air was a little fresher but not so cool that it was uncomfortable.

While Dad sat back and relaxed, Poppy decided to walk around the lawn and have a good sniff before settling beside his feet.

The rabbits had been out on the lawn again, their scent was very strong. One day she hoped to play with them, but if they were anything like the rabbits back home then every time she got close, they'd run away.

The pigs were now settled in their beds, as was the goat. Poppy looked over at the empty field beyond. She guessed that Samson had already herded the sheep, ready for their night's sleep.

*He's so clever to be able to control all those sheep,* she thought. *I couldn't even control one.*

Everything was quiet and still. No one was around, everyone now settled for the night. After making one lap around the lawn with her nose to the floor, Poppy walked back to Dad. She settled by his feet and watched an owl fly into the wood. Tiny bats shot across the sky, also heading towards the trees.

*Not everyone is settled for the night,* she thought.

Poppy stared at the wood. Thankfully, she didn't sense anything out of the ordinary.

Maybe, there wasn't a wild, whistling dog lurking in there after all. Perhaps everyone at Buttercup Farm was safe from a wild animal attack. Could this all be a result of Poppy's overactive imagination? She hoped so.

With a contented sigh, she rested her chin on her paws and closed her eyes to the sound of Dad drinking coffee.

Poppy drifted off to sleep. She was back on the beach, only this time Samson wasn't running away from her. In her dream they were running together across the sand, their long legs keeping in step with each other. Stride for stride. Leap for leap. She held her head up high, proud to be in the company of such a clever and striking dog.

As they ran, other dogs stared at them. For once, she felt like a Woodville Retriever, like her dog-pawrents and grandpawrents.

Poppy was proud of her lineage. She came from a family of show dogs. One of her earliest memories was scrambling over her siblings and pushing her nose through the bars of their enclosure. She remembered seeing her mom, Wren, being groomed. Wren had long, silky white hair and her tail fanned out like, she remembered hearing the kind lady say, 'an angel's wing,' Poppy thought then how beautiful her mom was. She even remembered the room, decked in brightly coloured rosettes. And now, here she was, running alongside Samson and feeling every bit as graceful and proud as the other Woodville Retrievers.

This was a good dream. The best. Poppy sighed and stirred, but her dream was so wonderful that she didn't want it to end, so she flopped on her side and drifted back to sleep.

The creak of a chair woke her. She opened her eyes.

*Am I still at the beach? Where's Samson?*

Poppy lifted her head. She watched Dad rise from his chair. Bleary-eyed, she looked around, taking in the empty garden, the farm buildings, long driveway, the fencing and the forest. She yawned.

So she wasn't at the beach with Samson, running beside him, stride for stride. The other dogs had never looked on in admiration and she hadn't appeared as beautiful and graceful as her mom. Poppy groaned.

'Come on, Pop,' Dad said, and walked towards the cottage.

Poppy noticed the light was fading. The lights were on inside, making it look even cosier and more inviting. She stood up and stretched, first flexing her back legs as she yawned again, her long tongue rolling out past her chin. She groaned. Then she stretched her front legs, bowing her head down and raising her bottom, curling her tail up and over her back like a creamy white sail.

Before joining the rest of her family inside and settling down for the night, Poppy took one more look at the wood. Everything was in near blackness, but it still wasn't so dark that she couldn't see the wild, overgrown greenery leading up to and into the trees.

Wildflowers swayed. Leaves rustled and sighed. If there was one thing Poppy had it was a keen sense of hearing.

Paws scurried over dry ground, stones and leaves. She waited, looking for the familiar white flash from the bobbed tail of a rabbit. There it was, weaving between the bushes. A big flash.

That was a big tail. Poppy stared. Come to think of it, what she had seen wasn't white at all. It looked more cream, or was it gold? Then again, it could have been a light brown...

The bushes shook. Twigs snapped. Poppy gulped.

She was certain that what she was seeing was no rabbit. She took a step forward, but then her nerve gave out.

*What was that?*

She remembered the white stag in Childer's Forest back home. But, catching sight of the flash of fur again, she decided this was too small to be a stag, and it was the wrong colour.

Poppy knew all the animals that lived in Childer's Forest. She thought about each one: robin, buzzard, mouse, rat, rabbit, squirrel, badger, fox, deer, stag, woodpecker... but this creature was none of those. Besides, she knew each of their scents, and what she smelt now was different.

Suddenly, everything fell still again. The flowers, leaves, grass, ferns, nettles – they were all motionless. Poppy felt her skin tingle. She had a strong sense of being watched. Eyes were peering, staring back at her, of this she was certain.

Once again, she thought back to the safari park. Back then, she had frozen in terror as she stared into the eyes of an African Wild Dog. She remembered it snarling at her: its big, yellowing fangs, long and sharp; teeth that could easily tear the flesh from her bones.

Right now, she recognised the same feeling. Relying on her senses, Poppy was in no doubt as to what was lurking and now spying on her in the wood. This was not a product of an overactive imagination. She was certain that what lay in wait was none other than a dhole – an Indian Wild Dog.

She heard the goat moving around in its enclosed shelter. Poppy's stomach gave a sickening jolt. She had a horrible thought…

The goat! The pigs, the hens, Olde Red, the Briggs family, Oliver and Olive, Bow, Samson, her own family – the Robinsons! No one was safe.

Poppy needed to do something, but what?

Dad stood on the doorstep, calling her.

Stealing one last glance at the wood, Poppy turned and raced to the safety of the cottage. Once the door was firmly closed behind her, she ran upstairs and settled in front of the window. From there she stared out at the wood, deciding what to do next.

*How did I escape the pack of wild dogs at the safari park?*
*I had help. Help from someone no one would dare argue with.*
*But that certain someone isn't here – if only he was…*

None of this was helping. She needed to tell someone before the dhole attacked. Poppy whined at the thought of the danger and of one of them falling victim.

Then she had a perfect idea.

*Who is the bravest and smartest on the farm?*

*Samson.*

Poppy's eyes grew heavy as she decided that, in the morning, she would find Samson and warn him of the danger.

# WARNING! DANGER!

It was another warm and sunny day.

Poppy stepped outside and looked around. She saw Dad talking to the pigs. For a moment, she considered joining them, but then noticed the wood.

In the calm light of day, the place didn't seem so threatening. *Maybe I'm imagining things*, she thought. *There are always a lot of animals living in a wood – just like the big forest back home. What I saw could be anything, not necessarily a wild dog.*

Poppy snorted and sneezed then stared out towards the trees. She narrowed her eyes, trying to detect movement from between the broad trunks.

*But what if I'm right? What if there is a blood-thirsty wild dog on the loose? What if it attacked the farm and I hadn't warned anyone?*

Poppy gulped. Her stomach clenched and she shivered. *It's no good. I can't take the chance. I have to find Samson and warn him of the danger. But where is he?*

Poppy couldn't see the collie anywhere. She hesitated for a moment, unsure of what to do. She took a step towards the wood.

*I'll have to investigate myself.* She remembered her day at the safari park. The day she and her new furriend were surrounded by wild dogs.

Poppy whined, recalling the fear and the danger. The evil glint in the snarling dogs' eyes. Their stained and sharp-looking teeth. The deep menacing growls and saliva that dripped from their jaws. Those dogs were ready for the kill. Did she really want to come face to face with one again?

The pigs were grunting and following Dad up and down the fence.

'Pigs… pigs… pigs.'

Dad chuckled. 'Is that so?' he said.

Poppy tilted her head.

*Can he really understand what the pigs are saying?*

But when Dad leaned over the fence and started talking about the weather, she guessed he had no clue either. He was just being polite.

Poppy looked back at the trees. Her stomach clenched. *I need to find Samson.*

Just then, Colin's truck pulled up outside the gate. Poppy couldn't believe her luck. Samson was bound to be there. She jumped up and barked, 'Samson! Samson!' then licked Colin's hand.

'Hello there, Poppy,' Colin said and ruffled her ears.

Dad stood beside her and patted her gently on the shoulder. This was Dad's way of telling her to settle down. So Poppy sat at his feet. This was hard to do, though, considering a dhole was lurking in the wood. She looked at the back of the truck. It was empty. Where were the collies?

'It'll be nice down on the beach today,' Colin said.

'Well, that's our plan. Make the most of this weather.'

Poppy's heart rose. Thoughts of ice cream and hotdogs filled her mind. She licked her lips.

'Our Flo will be down there with Samson,' Colin said. Poppy's ears quivered at the mention of his name. She remembered her plan to tell Samson about the wild dog and from there to find some way to warn Colin Briggs of the danger.

Poppy was positive there was a wild dog lurking in the wood, it was only a matter of time before the beast would strike.

'Samson!' Poppy barked, 'I must see Samson!'

Dad and Colin laughed.

'Yes, that's right, Pop, we're going to the beach,' Dad said, misinterpreting her frantic barks.

Poppy sighed.

She looked around and noted the sturdy fences and wire netting keeping the animals safe and secure.

*Perhaps they'll be all right,* Poppy thought, *until Samson and I can warn everyone.*

'We'll probably see Flo and Samson down at the beach,' Poppy heard Dad say.

'Oh yes, bound to,' Colin said. 'She's got to keep the old boy busy, you see. Samson isn't one for being idle. Bow will be joining me out on the field today.'

Before Poppy could process what Colin had said, she heard Jack and Evie. They were climbing into the car.

There wasn't a moment to lose. Poppy raced over and leapt inside. She sniffed Evie's lap. Where was Buttercup?

Jack giggled. 'She's looking for Buttercup.'

'Aw… you missing her, Poppy?' Evie said, stroking the top of Poppy's head. 'Mom, can I go back and get her?'

Mom looked over her shoulder at Evie as she fastened her seatbelt. 'No, Evie. Remember what I said. You don't want her getting wet and covered in sand. You don't want to risk losing her either. She'll be safer at the cottage.'

Poppy grumbled.

*Why should Buttercup be spared the water?* This didn't seem fair to her. Come to think of it, she didn't think it fair that Buttercup spent the night on Evie's bed either.

'We'll try the sea again, shall we, Pops?' Jack said, patting her on the shoulder.

'No,' Poppy growl-howled.

Dad climbed into the car.

'And what are you bleating about, Poppy?' he said as he started the engine.

'Jack's telling Poppy we're taking her into the sea again.'

Dad laughed. 'We'll see,' he said. 'She didn't seem too pleased last time.'

'Finally!' Poppy howled. 'They've got the message!'

# WHAT A DAY!

By the time the Robinsons arrived at the beach, it was still morning. The crowds had yet to arrive.

They settled by a cluster of rocks. Mom laid towels out on the sand and Dad tackled the parasol. Mom took bottles of water from the cooler and handed them around.

Poppy sat and tipped her head back, letting Evie pour the cool water into her mouth. That was better. Now feeling fully refreshed, she looked up and down the beach. Some families had already settled in their deckchairs – some behind windbreakers or beneath colourful parasols. Others played ball games, which Poppy longed to join.

She was pleased to see there were only a few people in the water.

*Maybe this'll be a day of ball games and no splashing about in the sea?* She hoped so.

She lifted her chin and filled her lungs with sea air. As she exhaled, long and slow, her gaze fell upon a handsome dog running across the sand in long fluid movements. It was Samson.

As he ran beside Flo, Poppy could tell he was deliberately holding back, making sure she kept up with him.

A few dogs waded into the water. Some were jumping and barking excitedly around their owners' legs. Samson ignored them.

Poppy thought back to her dream. She remembered running beside him. She'd looked so graceful and elegant, like a typical Woodville Retriever. She also remembered how she had felt being in Samson's company – happy, honoured, thrilled.

*That's it! What better way to attract Samson's attention than to behave like a Woodville?*

Poppy was eager to get going. She noticed the football lying on the sand next to Jack, who was kicking off his trainers and socks.

Poppy dived for the ball. Her jaws firmly clamped shut around the red and white leather. Her fangs sank between the stitching, ensuring the ball was firmly in place. Then, with a cheeky glance over her shoulder, she broke into a trot.

With another look over her shoulder to check Dad, Jack and Evie were following, she gained speed – but not too much – just enough to encourage them to keep up.

Samson was just ahead, still running alongside Flo. Now was her chance to make her move.

Poppy ran faster. She glanced back. Her family were going the wrong way! They called to her as they ran – but Poppy wouldn't follow. She couldn't because they were heading towards the sea.

Her plan was going all wrong.

She glanced at Samson. He wasn't too far ahead, but he wasn't looking in her direction either.

Poppy looked at Dad, Jack and Evie. They were very close to the water now. They kept calling her, beckoning her to join them.

Quickly, before her plan unravelled before her eyes, Poppy decided to try and intercept her family. She'd distract them with the ball and remind them that they were supposed to be playing one of her favourite games – chase me.

Poppy ran, still holding the ball firmly in her mouth. She turned quickly. Her family were changing direction again. She growled in frustration and started to race after them, but something caught her legs. She heard a growl – or was it her own? – and then she stumbled, dropping the ball as she went.

She tucked her head under as she tumbled, her legs thrashing about in the air. She jumped back on her feet. Her head shot up. She looked around, hoping no one had noticed.

She jumped backwards, feeling something graze her leg. Looking down, she saw a Yorkshire terrier growling angrily at her.

'Look where you're going!' he snarled, showing his teeth and snapping at her legs again.

Poppy tried dodging out of his way but the terrier was cross and in no mood to let matters lie.

'Sorry,' she grunted, trying her best to keep cool and calm. She looked around and was horrified to see Samson watching.

As if matters couldn't get any worse, an elderly lady approached. She had a thunderous expression on her face and waved her arms around violently.

'Get! Get!' she shouted, her face flushed. 'Go on, get away with you. You bad dog. Go on, shoo!'

She whisked the Yorkshire terrier up in her arms and turned away from Poppy, as though shielding the small dog from her. Poppy didn't know why, the terrier looked more than capable of defending himself.

The woman turned back to Poppy, her eyes blazing. She stepped towards her, using her free arm to push her away. Poppy swung around and ran – only what she hoped would be a quick escape ended in her tripping over a rock.

Poppy lost her balance and then… SPLASH!

She stood up slowly, her paws submerged in water. Seaweed clung to her coat.

'I'm really sorry,' Dad said, running over to Poppy, the angry lady and her bad-tempered dog.

Jack and Evie took Poppy by the collar.

She heard the woman talking to Dad and could tell by the tone of her voice that she wasn't happy. Meanwhile, the Yorkshire terrier still glared at her.

'Flippin' retrievers!' it snarled and yapped.

Poppy grumbled, then shook the water and seaweed off her coat. She forced herself to check if Samson was still there. He was.

She whimpered as she watched Flo nudge Samson, and then run back up the beach.

Samson gave Poppy one last look before turning away and following Flo into the distance.

# COULD THIS DAY GET ANY WORSE?

Poppy sat in the back of the car. She stuck her head out of the window, feeling the cool breeze blowing across her face. She closed her eyes, trying to blot out memories of that awful morning. The car sped down the road causing her ears and jowls to wobble. It felt nice and cheered her up a bit – but *only* a bit.

*What a day…*

She trembled, remembering the beach and her head-over-paws tumble, her legs kicking in the air.

'So much for the grace and elegance of a Woodville Retriever,' she grumbled.

She felt she'd let the Woodville name down. Why

couldn't she be more regal like the other Woodvilles'? She hated being clumsy and – even worse – she hated making a fool of herself.

Poppy rested her chin on the edge of the window. Her jowls wobbled. The touch of the cool air against her teeth felt quite nice. Then she felt Evie's little hand gently stroking her back.

Slowly, Poppy's bad mood eased. She was in Devon with her family. There was no school or work to take them away from her, and there were still days left of the holiday – plenty of time for her to tell Samson about the wild dog and save the farm from an imminent attack.

Poppy wagged her tail and licked Evie's hand before turning back to the window.

Once at the cottage, Mom stepped out of the car and opened the gate. Poppy heard the crackle and pop from the stones as the car moved slowly up the drive.

The pigs grunted cheerfully at them, their faces pressed together and snouts squeezed between the wire fence.

When Mom opened the back door, Poppy leapt down and ran over to the pigs.

They pressed their snouts towards her with a succession of short, cheerful grunts. 'Pigs, pigs, pigs.'

'How was your day?' Poppy barked, hoping they wouldn't reply by snorting, *Dhole! Whistling dog! Wild dog!* Thankfully, they didn't.

'Pigs. Pigs,' they grunted cheerfully.

Poppy sighed with relief. She trotted back and forth, and the pigs followed. She jumped backwards, lowered her chin to the ground and barked.

'Pigs!' the pigs grunted.

Poppy jumped forward and barked again. Even though she couldn't understand what the pigs were saying, she could see they were just as pleased to see her as she was to see them. She edged closer. The pigs did too until the three of them touched noses.

Poppy barked in surprise. Their snouts felt soft and warm. The pigs' eyes twinkled and they seemed to smile at her.

Poppy was so happy she spun in circles then zoomed around the lawn. Lap after lap, faster and faster she ran. Louder and louder she growled. She could hear the pigs calling to her, and from the corner of her eye, she saw them running up and down the fence.

Poppy was having so much fun she forgot about her disastrous morning – *I mean, the day couldn't possibly get any worse.*

Just as she stopped to catch her breath, she heard a scream coming from the cottage. Everyone was now inside. The windows were open, and Poppy's keen ears could tell that Evie's cry was not a happy one – something was seriously wrong.

# POPPY TO THE RESCUE

Poppy ran into the cottage. She heard Mom in the children's bedroom. Poppy peered around the door and saw Mom sat on the bed. She was cuddling Evie while her daughter sobbed on her shoulder.

'What's happened?' Poppy whimpered. She turned, hearing Dad and Jack running down the stairs.

'Well, she's not upstairs,' Dad said.

'She's not here either,' Jack's voice echoed from the bathroom.

Poppy was confused. She hated seeing anyone in her family sad. Whatever was wrong, she wanted to help. She pressed her nose into Evie's lap and rested her chin on the little girl's knees.

Mom looked down at her and smiled sadly.

Evie said something, but her face was pressed against Mom's chest so Poppy couldn't hear what it was. Evie's sobs grew louder. Poppy felt helpless. Only a few moments ago everything had been normal. Evie had even helped lift Poppy out of her bad mood. But now, Evie was broken-hearted and neither Poppy nor her mom could cheer her up.

Poppy sat at their feet and waited to hear what had happened. She heard Dad and Jack walk outside and then the sound of the car doors opening and closing.

Evie pulled herself away from Mom and gave a long, shuddering breath. Mom took a tissue out of her pocket and gently wiped Evie's eyes.

'We'll find her,' Mom said quietly. 'She can't have gone far.'

Evie gave a deep sigh, her shoulders rising then falling heavily.

'She was right here, Mom.'

'Yes, but did you take her upstairs with you after breakfast?'

Evie shook her head then scrunched her eyes.

'I don't know!' she sobbed as plump tears rolled from her eyes and down her cheeks.

Poppy suddenly had an idea who'd gone missing. She felt guilty about her previous thoughts, her feelings of resentment at what seemed like favouritism towards the newest member of the family.

And as if to confirm Poppy's theory, Evie then cried, 'Buttercup!'

Poppy turned and ran. She ran through the front door, across the lawn and towards the fence. As she approached, the goat turned towards her.

'I'm sorry to bother you,' Poppy whimpered, 'but we've lost Buttercup. You haven't seen her, have you?'

The goat stared at her. Its ears and tail twitched and flicked at the annoying flies buzzing around.

Poppy was about to repeat her question when the goat stepped forward.

'No. No one,' she bleated, her jaw constantly moving, chomping. 'You can try asking those two over there.' She nodded towards the farmhouse.

'OK. Thank you,' Poppy barked, and then ran towards the farmhouse.

She didn't hold out much hope for Olive and Oliver. They'd only ever been rude to her. If it wasn't for Bow, then all the dogs on Buttercup Farm would be unapproachable. Still, Buttercup was missing and Evie was distraught. Regardless of her feelings, Poppy had to try anyone who might have seen or heard anything.

She trotted up to the gate that led to the front door of the farmhouse. There, stretched out in front of the doorstep, were Oliver and Olive. Both lay on their backs warming their bellies in the sun.

Olive wriggled deeper into her fluffy bed and snored loudly. Her back leg twitched as though scratching an invisible flea. She snorted over and over again. For a moment, Poppy thought something was seriously wrong with the pug, but then Olive stopped and lifted her head. She opened one eye and peered at Poppy, her front paw bent over her nose.

Poppy took a step forward. She watched Olive rock from side to side, trying to gain leverage, before swinging on to her paws.

'Poppy, right?' Olive growled.

'Yes. I'm hoping you can help me,' Poppy whined. 'Have you seen Buttercup? She's gone missing.'

Olive frowned, making the wrinkles that ran across her squashed face even deeper.

'Who's Buttercup?'

'She's Evie's puppy from the holiday fairy. She looks like me only smaller.'

Before Olive could answer, Oliver snorted loudly. He stretched his back leg, then broke wind. It was so loud that he woke himself up.

Poppy was horrified, but Olive didn't seem to notice.

'What's going on?' Oliver grunted, his voice still croaky from sleep.

'It's that retriever,' Olive barked, glancing down at him as he slowly rolled off his bed. 'The family next door have lost a dog. Its name's Buttercup.'

'She looks like me only smaller. She's only a puppy,' Poppy added, trying not to feel too offended at being called '*that retriever*'.

Oliver stared at her. His nose twitched, then he sneezed. He shook his head. His pointy ears reminded Poppy of the pictures she'd seen of bats. The thought of bats reminded Poppy of those she saw flying into the wood. Her stomach turned.

*The wood. Oh no. The dhole!*

'Have you seen her?' Poppy barked. It was her loudest I'm-annoyed-now bark, and she hoped it would alert them to the seriousness of the situation.

Despite Oliver being a fraction of Poppy's size, he seemed neither concerned nor scared of her. He pulled his shoulders back and looked her in the eye.

'No, I haven't, but you could ask Samson.'

'And good luck with that,' Olive growled. They caught each other's eyes and howled.

Poppy turned away. She was getting nowhere with these two, and besides, there was no time to waste. Poor Buttercup was lost and alone somewhere.

*This has been the worst day ever*, Poppy thought as she walked away from Oliver and Olive. The sound of their howling laughter carried around the farmyard.

The wood. If Buttercup wasn't in the cottage, the car or anywhere in the farmyard then that was the only place she could be.

Over the last few days, Poppy had grown to fear the wood, or rather what was lurking inside it. But now, with her heart pounding and legs shaking, she ran towards the trees, barking at the top of her voice, 'Buttercup! Buttercup!'

# STRANGE NOISES AND DARK SHADOWS

It was cold in the wood. Sunlight struggled to squeeze through the trees. Poppy stood in one of the few pools of light, hoping to warm up.

She shivered. *Was this the cold or was it fear? Surely it shouldn't be so cold on a sunny day in August?*

She thought about how hot it had been at the beach, then quickly put all memories of that disastrous morning behind her.

Something moved. A twig snapped. Poppy gulped. Her body shook.

What would she do if she came face to face with the dhole? Poppy had no idea, but thinking of Evie, upset and heartbroken – not to mention Buttercup – left her in no doubt as to what she *must* do.

'Buttercup!' she barked again, slicing through the eerie stillness that lay across the wood. With her nose pressed to the floor, she ventured farther.

It didn't take long for her to detect the smell which was now all too familiar. The scent of dhole.

Poppy ran.

She leapt over rocks, ploughed through clusters of wildflowers and nettles, jumped over large twisted exposed roots. Her senses were alert. Her eyes were everywhere. Despite her fear, she knew she had to find Buttercup before the wild dog did.

'Buttercup!' she barked as she wove in between the trees – the unnatural stillness had now lifted.

Something rustled above her. She looked up to see a squirrel peering down from the safety of its branch. It chattered angrily but Poppy ignored it. She had more important things on her mind.

The smell was getting stronger. Her stomach clenched in dread at what she might find.

Poppy whimpered. *I hope Buttercup's all right.*

Ferns rustled. Wildflowers swayed. Poppy turned sharply, her ears picking up every sound around her: birds singing, their wings beating, squirrels scampering, bees buzzing, leaves rustling… someone breathing.

Poppy's heart began to pound so fast she had trouble barking.

'Hello? Buttercup? Is that you?' *Crikey* – she thought – *my voice is so wobbly I sound like Olde Red the cockerel.*

She knew she was being watched, but by whom? The bush in front of her swayed. She caught her breath and stared at the pair of eyes peering at her through the bracken.

The figure was small, much too small to be a wild dog. She noticed glimpses of orangey-gold through the leaves. Poppy sighed. Relieved.

'Buttercup, there you are.'

She stepped closer, careful not to frighten the puppy further.

'Come on,' she growled softly, 'I'll take you back to Evie. She's missing you.'

Buttercup stepped out from behind the bracken. She tilted her head to one side, making her ears flop and flap against her face.

*The poor love is confused and afraid,* Poppy thought, then stepped closer and gently pressed her nose against Buttercup's muzzle. In return, the little one leant in to greet her. Poppy whined, feeling her tremble.

'It's OK,' Poppy growled softly. 'I've found you now.'

Buttercup looked up at Poppy and whined. 'Will you take me home?'

'Of course,' Poppy groaned and licked her large, floppy ears.

*That's funny. I didn't realise how big her ears were,* Poppy thought. *Not to mention their colour. The sun must have burned them because they're almost red.*

She nuzzled against one of those reddish-golden ears, hoping her actions would help calm Buttercup, but instead she felt the little one tense up.

Then Poppy heard it too.

Someone was coming.

Poppy's relief at finding Buttercup alive and well had distracted her from the dhole. But the scent was still lingering, getting stronger in fact and that's why she knew what was coming.

Determined to hide her fear from Buttercup, Poppy nudged her and growled softly.

'This way, come on.' She ran down the twisting narrow path, checking that Buttercup was following.

Her legs shook, her heart was beating so fast she struggled to breathe. She hadn't felt this afraid since the safari park.

The pounding of paws on the dry leafy floor grew faster and louder. The dhole was gaining on them and there was nothing Poppy could do but turn and face it.

Without a moment's hesitation, Poppy pushed Buttercup into the bushes.

'Stay there and keep quiet!' she growled then spun around.

There was no time to falter. Poppy needed to act fast before fear took over. She curled her lip back and snarled. She barked, her heckles rising.

'Go away!' she snarled. 'Get back.'

# SEARCH AND RESCUE

Twigs and branches snapped. Leaves rustled. In a moment Poppy and Buttercup would come face to face with the dhole.

Poppy gulped, swallowing back the whimper of fear that was forming in her throat.

Suddenly, the bushes were pushed aside and a large dark figure leapt out in front of them.

'Samson!' Poppy barked, 'What are you doing here?'

The collie skidded to a halt. He looked at her, his chest rising and falling steadily.

Samson growled, 'I heard Evie crying and saw you running into the wood. I was worried and wondered if I could help.'

Poppy was stunned. First Evie was heartbroken, then Poppy found Buttercup, then they were being chased by a wild dog, and now Samson stood before them, not just offering to help, but actually being nice.

Poppy shook her head, trying to think clearly. Fortunately, she couldn't hear the dhole anymore. Samson must have frightened it off.

'I've found Buttercup,' she growled proudly. 'That's why Evie was upset, we'd lost her. But…' Poppy groaned quietly and took a step closer, 'we need to be careful.' She looked around cautiously.

She lifted her head slightly, looking over Samson's shoulder. She growled, her lips barely moving, 'There's a dhole in the wood,'

She stepped closer to Samson, hoping to be out of Buttercup's earshot. Samson's ear twitched as Poppy's nose brushed his cheek. He probably didn't know what a dhole was, but now wasn't the time to explain.

'It's following us,' she grunted. 'We need to go to the farm and get Buttercup back to Evie.'

Poppy lifted her head and nodded discreetly back to the bush where Buttercup was hiding. 'She's in there.

But we need to keep calm. We mustn't show her that we're afraid.'

Samson glanced over her shoulder to the bush, then back to Poppy.

*Samson's good at hiding his fear,* Poppy thought. *Even with a dhole spying on us, he stays cool and calm.*

He stepped back and looked around, then turned back to her.

'Poppy, there are no wild dogs around here, except in a safari park.'

Poppy was surprised. *So Samson does know what a dhole is. Was there anything this wise collie didn't know?*

'It could have escaped,' she growled, but Samson shook his head.

'No, Poppy. I can assure you there's no dhole. I walk through this wood every day and if there was one, believe me, I'd have sniffed it out and warned Colin.'

Poppy took a deep breath and sighed. 'Well, that's a relief,' she barked. 'But I'm sure I smelt a wild dog.'

Samson frowned. 'That's strange because I can't.'

'Samson, there's a scent about this wood that is not a forest smell.'

The collie lifted his head and sniffed the air. He peered at the bush behind Poppy.

'Buttercup? You can come out now,' Poppy barked.

Buttercup gingerly stepped out into the open. She looked up at Samson.

'It's OK,' Poppy growled and walked over to her.

She could see how afraid she was of the huge black and white collie. 'Samson's going to help.'

Buttercup didn't answer.

Meanwhile, the collie looked from Buttercup to Poppy.

'This isn't Buttercup,' he growled.

The puppy sat down and watched the two big dogs, her head turning from left to right.

'Of course it is,' Poppy barked. 'I'd know Buttercup anywhere. I think I know her better than you, Samson.'

Poppy wasn't going to let Samson think she was wrong for a second time. So far today, nothing had gone right. To be proved wrong yet again – and by Samson – was too much.

Samson took a deep breath and lowered his head to Buttercup's level.

'Little one,' he ruffed, deeply and softly, 'is your name Buttercup?'

Buttercup looked up at Samson and then back to Poppy. Her big brown eyes glistened.

'She's only been with us for a few days,' Poppy explained. 'She's not used to her name yet.'

Samson sat down and looked at Poppy. 'Have you ever heard Buttercup bark?'

The puppy stood up and stepped back.

'Have you ever seen Buttercup stand up by herself?' Samson continued.

Buttercup backed into the bush and cowered. She growled and groaned.

'Have you heard Buttercup growl?'

Poppy thought for a moment. She remembered all the times Buttercup had lain on Evie's bed or joined them in the car – she'd either lie on Evie's lap or was tucked under her arm.

'Poppy,' Samson growled softly. He stepped towards her. 'Buttercup is a soft toy. This here is a real puppy.'

Poppy was confused. *Surely Samson's wrong?*

Yet, as she watched the puppy she had thought was Buttercup walk cautiously up to them, its tail wagging, she had to admit Samson was right.

She whined at the sad and confused look in its eyes.

The Buttercup she knew always had the same fixed expression on her face. Come to think of it, Buttercup never made a sound. Sometimes, the pup's silence annoyed her. It wasn't nice being ignored. And yet, Poppy realised, she wasn't being ignored at all!

'Do you have a name?' Poppy whined, deliberately keeping her voice soft and gentle, hoping not to frighten the little one.

The puppy shook its head. 'I don't think so. But I'd like to go home now.' Its sad eyes tugged at Poppy's heartstrings.

'You look like my mom,' the pup whimpered. 'I've been watching you. At first, I thought you were her, but then I wasn't so sure.'

This explained Poppy's feeling of being watched.

'How did you get here?' Samson barked, still keeping his voice low and soft.

Poppy noticed the change in the pup's expression. The little one took a deep breath and frowned with concentration.

'I remember being in bed. It was warm and cosy,' she whined, then continued, 'A monster came. It had bright eyes and its roar…'

Poppy caught her breath. *Monster?* She didn't like the sound of that.

'Dhole!' she barked, forgetting to hide her fear. She scanned the trees around them.

'No, Poppy. There's no dhole here,' Samson growled.

'But she said a monster…' Poppy's voice trailed away. They exchanged looks. Poppy hadn't a clue what the puppy meant and, judging by the expression on Samson's face, neither did he.

'I just want to go home,' the puppy whined.

Everyone was deep in thought until Samson barked. 'Poppy, you stay here while I fetch help.'

Poppy wasn't too happy being alone with pup while there was a monster on the loose. But for the moment, she didn't sense any danger. She lay down and the pup curled up beside her.

They watched Samson run back through the wood. Poppy knew it wouldn't be long now until either her family or Colin came for them.

# PUPPY

Poppy licked the pup's ears. She pulled out the bits of leaves and brambles that were tangled in its reddish-golden tufts.

'So, Pup, you don't have a name?'

The puppy shook her head but then she suddenly stopped. Poppy saw the recognition in the little one's expression.

'I've been called little girl before. Perhaps that's my name?'

Poppy doubted that.

'OK. Well, for now, I'll call you Pup. Is that OK?'

The little one nodded.

'Can you tell me about your mom?'

She felt Pup take a deep, shuddering breath. In an attempt to comfort her, Poppy pressed her wet nose against the top of her head.

'You remind me of her. She's big, warm and fluffy like you. There were a lot of us. We were all together, clambering over one other to get to Mom's milk. When we got a bit older, Mom had a bed of her own and we puppies stayed together. One by one, the others went away until I was left on my own.

'I still have my comfy bed, though. It smells of my mom and that makes me feel better.'

Poppy rested her chin beside Pup's face.

'And then you ended up here?'

'I've been called a nosey pup before,' the little one said, then its face brightened. 'Maybe that's my name? Nosey Pup.'

Poppy sighed. 'It could be. But I prefer just Pup, don't you?'

Pup nodded.

'I got bored lying in bed, so I decided to have a look around. Then the monster came.'

Something didn't sound right to Poppy.

She raised her head and watched Pup nibbling her little paw. She wondered who – or what – this monster was. She sniffed the air trying to detect its scent, but the only unfamiliar smell was what she had mistaken to be dhole. Now, she knew the scent had belonged to – Pup.

'It sounds like your siblings went to new homes,' Poppy growled softly. 'It was the same for me. I guess no house is big enough to keep a whole litter of goldie pups, especially when fully grown.' She paused, thinking back to when her forever family had collected her. That first night, she remembered missing her siblings, but, with Mom and Dad's reassurance, she soon settled in.

'So, Pup, were you introduced to your new hoomans?'

Pup tilted her head.

'People,' Poppy explained. 'Did some people come and take you to your new home?'

Pup's mouth and nose twitched from side to side as she thought. Eventually, she shook her head.

'No,' she yapped, then yawned.

'You've had a busy day,' Poppy growled. 'Settle down and rest. I'll wake you when Samson and the others get here.'

'Will the others take me home?' Pup's words were slow and got swallowed up in another long yawn.

Poppy pushed her muzzle against Pup's head, encouraging the little one to settle down.

'Don't worry,' Poppy grunted, 'we'll get you back

home. It sounds like the breeder decided to keep you; that happens a lot.'

Pup grunted then snorted.

'Your owners are probably out looking for you at this very moment.'

Pup was silent.

Poppy peered down to find the little one fast asleep.

# MEET THE ROBINSONS

For the first time that day, Poppy relaxed.

As she lay in the shade of the trees, she realised that she didn't feel cold anymore. It was a nice, comfortable temperature.

A sliver of golden sunlight lay across her paw and Pup's head as the puppy slept against her.

Poppy had so many questions. Now, in the peacefulness of the wood, with its familiar gentle sounds of small animals scampering through the undergrowth and trees rustling and sighing, Poppy was free to let her mind wander.

She was deep in thought, wondering where Pup came from, how desperate the owners must be, and also wondering if Evie had found Buttercup, when she heard movement up ahead.

Poppy recognised the sound of her family's footsteps, their voices and their scent. She could also hear the rapid thud of Samson's paws as he ran.

*At last, we can get Pup home*, Poppy thought. She stirred, rousing Pup from her nap.

'Pup, help is here.'

The puppy stood up. She leaned back, stretched and then gave a big yawn followed by a groan-squeak. She looked lost and confused, but Poppy soon saw the recognition return to her face, remembering and realising where she was.

'Come on,' Poppy whined, 'don't be afraid.' She licked Pup's face, then stood up just as Samson burst through a gap in the trees.

Dad and Carol were the first to appear, shortly followed by Mom, Jack and Evie. One of the first things Poppy noticed was Buttercup tucked safely under Evie's arm.

*Where's Buttercup been?* Poppy wondered, then realised it didn't matter; the main thing was that she had been found.

Evie was smiling once more and, Poppy noticed, her face lit up when she saw Pup.

'Who's this little fella?' Dad said as he crouched on the floor in front of them. He smiled and held out his hand for the little one to sniff. Pup reached over and licked the tips of his fingers.

'I have no idea,' Carol said softly, her face creased into a gentle smile. 'But she's gorgeous.' She turned to Samson and stroked the top of his head. 'Good boy.'

Jack and Evie knelt beside Poppy. They wrapped their arms around her. She could tell both were a little nervous. She guessed it was because neither wanted to frighten Pup, and also they were a little unsure themselves. Mom and Dad had always taught them to be cautious of dogs they didn't know.

Poppy decided to settle their unease by licking their arms and wagging her tail.

'My family will take care of you,' Poppy barked to Pup.

This made the hoomans laugh.

'Are you playing at being a mom?' Dad said and gently ruffled the top of both their heads.

Mom walked slowly towards them. She knelt down and talked softly to Pup. Poppy was thankful they spoke quietly and moved slowly, helping Pup feel at ease.

Poppy stole a glance at Samson. There was a twinkle in his eyes that revealed to Poppy a gentler side to his nature.

Mom reached over and picked Pup up. At first, Poppy was surprised by how anxious she felt seeing Pup being carried away.

'It's OK,' Mom said, reading Poppy's thoughts. She stood up, gently caressing Pup's big ears. 'Just look at those ears,' she said, smiling, 'they're huge!'

Poppy jumped up against Mom and licked Pup's paw.

Dad took hold of Poppy's collar. 'Hey,' he said calmly, 'settle down.'

Poppy felt calmer hearing the steady tone of his voice. She watched Mom and Carol fussing over Pup. Meanwhile, the puppy's tail beat against Mom's hip and she licked their fingers.

'Shall we take her back to the cottage?' Mom asked. She looked at Dad and then at Carol.

'Good idea,' said the farmer's wife, 'and while you do that I'll phone the vet. Once they've scanned her microchip we'll soon get her home.'

'We'll be with you in a bit,' Dad said as Mom and Carol turned away.

Samson turned to Poppy. He didn't make a sound but Poppy knew what he was thinking.

'Yes, I know Pup will be all right,' Poppy barked, 'I'm just making sure she's not frightened.'

She guessed Samson thought she was being silly again.

'She's only a puppy,' she barked, in case a further explanation was needed.

Samson dipped his head. Poppy was pleased by his acknowledgement. She felt she was salvaging what had started out as one of the worst days ever.

Mom and Carol were cooing and groaning – which was something Mom and Evie always did whenever they saw something cute and cuddly. Poppy heard the tiniest howl. This made her feel strangely warm and fuzzy. It sounded as if Pup was enjoying all the attention.

Samson ran after Carol, leaving Poppy with Dad, Jack, Evie and Buttercup. Evie made a move to run after Mom, but Dad stopped her.

He placed his hand on her shoulder and said, 'Best leave them to it for now, while they phone around. We need to find out where the puppy's come from. So…' he grinned, 'fancy a game of football?'

Poppy barked. 'Yes!'

She followed Mom and Carol. After a few paces, she turned back and barked again. 'Come on, hurry up!'

# GAME ON

When Poppy and Jack reached the lawn they found Samson lying in the sunshine. Except for the farm animals relaxing behind the fence, he was alone. There was no sign of Mom, Pup or Carol, so Poppy guessed they were in the cottage. She wanted to go inside too and see what was going on.

*What is a microchip? What will the vet do to Pup?* But she told herself that while Pup was in Carol and Mom's care, nothing bad could happen – so Poppy joined Samson.

Seeing the handsome dog looking at her, she suddenly felt self-conscious. She lifted her head, raised her tail so that the feathering swayed as she moved, and pranced over to him. Step by step, she scrutinised every movement she made. The sun shone on her cream coat, the heat felt nice against her fur and she hoped that at long last, Samson would see her in a better light.

*I'm a Woodville Retriever and proud of it,* she thought and nearly barked out loud but she corrected herself in time.

She heard Jack bouncing the football. Her ears twitched and her heartbeat quickened at the sound of it hitting the ground. Smack. Crunch. Smack. Crunch.

SMACK! The ball hit her across the back of the head.

Poppy stumbled, yet managed to keep her balance. She spun around, regaining her composure.

'Sorry, Poppy!' Jack said.

She glanced at Samson. 'I knew the ball was coming…' she quickly barked, then dashed after it. She bumped it with her nose and sent it rolling towards Samson.

He didn't move. He didn't charge and lunge, or head-butt the ball. Instead, he watched it roll towards him.

*What have I done now?* she thought, watching him look from the ball to her then back to the ball. She dipped her head and tried nudging it. It didn't work. She lost her balance and stumbled again, which made her cuss and growl irritably to herself.

Then, Jack was beside her. This made her feel less self-conscious. She raced beside him, barking as he dribbled the ball.

'Pass it. Pass it,' she barked.

Jack dodged around her, keeping control of the football. Then, when Dad and Evie appeared, he kicked it to them. Poppy ran full pelt, barking as she went. Dad stopped the ball with his foot and tapped it to Evie.

'Pass it. Pass it,' Poppy barked again. She stood in front of Evie, tail up, head down, – determined to impress Samson.

Evie giggled as she kicked the ball. Poppy swooped. She head-butted the ball and opened her mouth ready to seize it, but her jaws snapped thin air.

She grumbled, 'Come here,' then butted the ball again. It rolled across the lawn past Samson.

Poppy spun around. She was about to charge but stopped when she saw Samson staring at the football.

She didn't understand. Had that been her, she'd have been on her feet waiting for an opportunity to steal the ball and join in the fun.

'Samson!' she barked, 'Come on!'

He stared at her. At first, she thought her behaviour was annoying him, but when she stepped closer she realised she was wrong.

The proud dog seemed confused. He looked at the ball and tilted his head. He looked at Poppy, then back at the ball again.

'Come on, Samson,' Dad said as he jogged past. He looked across at the handsome collie-dog. 'Come on. Fetch.'

Samson wouldn't budge. Poppy couldn't believe it.

The perfect, proud and clever border collie didn't know what to do.

Poppy's focus shifted to the ball. She lowered her head and stared, waiting for Dad to kick it. When he did, she leapt up ready to catch it, but instead…

The ball bounced off her head.

'I meant to do that!' she barked hastily as she twisted in mid-air and raced after the bouncing football.

Jack and Evie went after the ball too, and so did Buttercup who was still firmly tucked beneath Evie's arm. As Jack stepped aside for his sister, Poppy skidded to a halt in front of her.

She barked and danced from paw to paw. 'Kick it. Kick it, Evie.'

Evie kicked the ball to Poppy. She caught it easily in her mouth and then the fun *really* began…

# LESSONS IN FUN

One of Poppy's favourite games was chase me, and now the chase was on.

With a sideways glance at Samson, Poppy trotted away, the ball held firmly in her mouth. Her body swayed and she wiggled her bottom.

If she could have barked, she'd have said, 'Look at me! The ball's mine now.' But she didn't dare let go of the ball.

Dad lunged towards her. Poppy dipped her head and changed direction quickly. As she swung around, Jack appeared in front of her. He opened his arms and grinned. Poppy swung herself to the right, her tail swaying with excitement.

She ran up to Samson, who was just sitting watching the fun.

She growled, nodding her head, with the ball still held securely in her mouth.

Samson pulled his head back and growled, 'What do you want me to do?'

Poppy dropped the ball. 'What do you mean?' She tilted her head.

'Do you want me to *come by* or *away*?'

'What? What are you on about, Samson?'

'When I'm herding the sheep, that's what I do.'

'But we're not herding sheep. We're not working, we're playing.'

Samson stood up and walked slowly around the football. He lowered his body to the ground. With his eyes fixed on the ball, he began stalking it.

'Samson,' Poppy growled, 'what are you doing?'

'What I always do, and what I do best,' he replied, still staring at the ball. He moved slowly. 'Where do you want the ball to go?'

Poppy hadn't got a clue what he was talking about. All she wanted was to play.

She jumped around and barked, 'Just grab it and run. Push it with your nose.'

'What? I don't understand,' Samson barked.

Jack and Evie joined them. As Jack kicked the ball away, the collie jumped. Poppy was amazed at how uncomfortable he looked.

She watched him running around Jack, Evie and the

ball. He ran in a wide circle, his eyes fixed on nothing but them. He was acting as though he was in the field with Colin. Poppy remembered watching him rounding up the sheep, skilfully driving them around the meadow.

'Samson!' she barked. 'You're not working now.'

Dad jogged over to Poppy. He patted her shoulder and laughed.

'Samson thinks you're a flock of sheep,' he said, watching Jack and Evie kicking the ball to each other while Samson ran in circles around them. 'Look, he's trying to round you up.'

Poppy couldn't believe that something as natural to her as a ball game was so strange and new to Samson. *Perhaps*, she realised, *he doesn't know everything after all?*

She ran over to him. 'Follow me,' she barked.

She intercepted the ball as Jack kicked it to Evie. She butted it with her nose and sent it rolling across the lawn.

'Go after it and push it with your nose,' she barked to Samson.

He did as he was told. She watched him race across the lawn, swoop down and knock the ball away with his nose.

'Like that?' he barked.

'Yes!' Poppy watched him race after the ball.

Dad joined in, and before long they were all playing a combination of football and chase me.

Playing games in the hot afternoon sun tired everyone out. Dad brought two bowls of water for Poppy and Samson and then he and the children went inside to eat their lunch.

Poppy lay in the shade of the barn and looked at the cottage. The front door was open and the hallway looked invitingly cool, but she was happy lying in the shade next to her new friend.

While Samson slept, she wondered about Mom and Pup. She hadn't noticed them leave the cottage so she guessed they were still inside. Perhaps she should go in and see how the little one was?

The moment Poppy stirred, Samson opened one eye.

'I'm going to see how Pup is,' she explained.

'Carol has driven them to the vets,' Samson growled. 'I saw them leave earlier.'

'I hope she'll be all right.'

'She'll be OK. It's better than fending for herself in the wood.'

'Samson, what's a microchip?' This was something that had niggled Poppy since hearing the word mentioned in the wood.

'It's like a tag that's injected into us. It holds our owner's details, so if we get lost, our families can be traced. Both you and I have one. You probably don't remember because you'd have been very young.'

Poppy looked at Samson. She liked the way he calmed her down with his knowledge, confidence and common sense.

'Did you enjoy the game?' She was eager to know what he thought, pleased to have seen a change in him, to see a side of Samson she had never witnessed before.

Samson stretched out in the sun. He yawned and looked back at her, his tail wagging.

'Yes, it was… fun.'

His hesitation made Poppy wonder if he'd ever had fun before.

# Through the Eyes of Others

It was a lazy, chilled-out afternoon at Buttercup Farm. Poppy found the usual chatter – the grunts, the clucking, quacking, even the geese honking – very soothing and relaxing.

She watched Samson stretch out beside her. He lay with his chin cradled between his paws, his breath slow and steady and his eyes closed. She'd never seen him so relaxed.

She looked around and noticed Oliver and Olive yawning and stretching before flopping back down on their beds. Best buddies, always together. Constantly side by side.

Poppy sighed. Her eyes grew heavy. It had been a busy and eventful day, and now she was tired too.

Just as she was drifting off to sleep, a whistle disturbed the quietness. Poppy's ears twitched and she lifted her head higher to see where the sound was coming from. Samson heard it too. He sat up and looked across the road. Poppy followed his stare and saw Colin working in the field with Bow.

The young collie responded to every whistle Colin made. She was quick, agile and obedient. But Poppy heard Samson's disapproving groans and sighs.

'Do you wish you were with them?' Poppy whined, watching Bow circling the sheep, then –following another sharp whistle from Colin – lie flat on her stomach.

'She's too unsure. The sheep can sense it. Look…'

Poppy watched as some of the flock broke away.

'I think she's doing well,' Poppy whined then pulled her ears back as Samson turned and gave her a stern look. She swallowed nervously. 'Both you and Bow are clever. I couldn't do that.'

Samson turned back to the field. Poppy watched him. His mood had changed, she could see and sense it. He stared at Colin and Bow. His eyes looked sad.

Eventually, Samson tore his eyes away and looked down at Poppy. 'Bow's my replacement,' he barked softly.

'Replacement?' Poppy sat up, her calm and relaxed mood now gone. 'Why? Where are you going?'

Samson shook his head. 'I don't know. Colin hasn't said.' He looked back at the field and watched Colin walk over to Bow. The young collie jumped up at him and he made a fuss of her.

Samson growled.

'You see, Poppy,' he kept staring at his owner and the excitable collie-dog, 'I've always been Colin's dog. I'm not a pet like Oliver and Olive – or you.'

Poppy looked across to the farmhouse. The pug and French bulldog snored and grunted in their sleep, their legs occasionally twitching.

'It's always been me and Colin,' Samson continued. 'I'm a working dog; I don't laze around and perform silly tricks to amuse the hoomans. I help Colin run the farm. But since Bow came along, I'm doing less and less. I spend more time watching Colin and Bow at work. With Bow around, Colin doesn't need me. If I'm not working with Colin, then what am I meant to do?'

This came as a shock to Poppy. She had thought Samson led the perfect, contented life. He appeared secure and in control, but now she realised she had been mistaken.

'You go to the beach with Flo,' she growled,

thinking this would please him, but he shook his head and snarled.

'That's just to get me out of the way. While I'm at the beach, Bow's with Colin doing my job.' She heard his low, deep growl as he watched Bow stalking the sheep. 'I'm happy where I should be, out on that field with Colin.' He nodded towards the farmer.

Poppy whined. She hated seeing Samson troubled.

'When I'm not out there I don't know what my purpose is. I'm a working dog – if I'm not working then what am I supposed to do?'

Poppy wished she could think of something to cheer him up and take his troubles away.

'I like being with Flo,' he continued. 'It's nice going out for a run, but it's not the same.' He lay down and tucked his paw beneath him. 'I wish I could relax and have fun like you. You make everyone around you happy. When I watch you on the beach, everything looks fun. How do you do it, Poppy?'

Poppy could hardly believe her ears. So, all those times on the beach, he hadn't been thinking badly of her – however angry or disgusted he'd seemed.

'I don't know, Samson,' she gruffed, 'I just have fun. It's hard not to on the beach, with all that sand and ice cream around.'

Samson howled suddenly , startling Poppy.

'Your face when you were lapping up that ice cream! There was more on your jowls than in your mouth,' he howled again. 'Everyone likes you. The ice cream man would have given you anything you wanted. I wish I had that effect on people.'

Poppy shook her head.. 'But what about that Yorkshire terrier?' she growled.

Samson dismissed her comment with a shake of his head. 'It takes all sorts,' he barked. 'There will always be one or two who are on the grumpy side. Ignore them, Poppy. They're not worth worrying about.'

'So, you don't think I'm silly, stupid and clumsy?'

Samson stared at her. He tilted his head from one side to the other.

Eventually, he barked, 'How could you think that? I'd love to be more like you. You enjoy life. You know how to have fun and you have this ability to make others around you happy. When I watch you on the beach, I'd give anything to be able to join in with you.'

Memories of her times at the beach flashed through Poppy's mind. The times Samson had stared at her, looking so stern and disapproving; not to mention that first day when she ran into him.

'But I'm clumsy, Samson! Remember that time when I crashed into you? And don't tell me you found that funny because you were annoyed, I could tell.'

The big collie shook his head.

'I'm sorry, Poppy,' he growled, 'but that's exactly what I mean. I can't have fun. I don't know how. OK, so you're a bit clumsy, but that's part of what makes you who you are; that's why everyone likes you.'

The farm animals continued their chatter, but Poppy

didn't hear them. A whole pack of dholes could have been rampaging through the wood, and she wouldn't have noticed because Samson had said he liked her just the way she was!

# JUST A BIG SOFTIE

As Carol's car pulled up outside the cottage, Poppy and Samson ran over to greet them. But when Mom and Carol climbed out of the car, Poppy's tail fell still.

*Where is Pup?*

Poppy and Samson exchanged looks before following them into the cottage.

Dad, Jack and Evie ran down the stairs to meet them.

'Everything OK?' Dad asked. He was smiling, but Poppy saw the concern in his eyes.

'The vet's keeping the puppy at the surgery,' Mom said. She heard Evie and Jack gasp and groan in protest, but she silenced them with a shake of her head and said, 'Don't worry, she's all right.'

Carol stepped forward. 'The vet checked her over and she's in perfect health. The problem is she hasn't been microchipped, so we can't return her to her owners – yet.'

Poppy frowned. *Not microchipped?*

Samson sat down beside Carol whilst Poppy's mind wandered.

'... The vet said she'd make a few enquiries and contact the police. Someone might have reported her missing.' Carol smiled at Samson. 'Right then,' she said to the collie, clasping her hands together and rubbing them vigorously. 'I'd best get your dinner, hadn't I?'

Samson stood up and wagged his tail. He barked – one clear, loud bark that made everyone smile. Seeing this, Samson's tail wagged even faster.

The Robinsons walked back upstairs – but Poppy didn't join them.

She sat outside and stared at the trees, thinking back to when she had first found the puppy. If Evie's Buttercup hadn't gone missing, would she have found Pup at all? She wouldn't have ventured that far into the wood, that's for sure. Not while she thought a dhole was on the prowl.

*Just how long had Pup been in there? And why hasn't she been microchipped? Did her owners forget?*

Poppy growled, wondering how the little one was – alone again in another strange place.

The thought of Pup lying in a cage lonely and afraid made Poppy feel useless.

Poppy whined again, and moments later Mom and Jack stepped outside.

'Poppy?' Jack said, then sat on the floor beside her and gently stroked her back. 'What's wrong?'

Poppy licked his hand. She looked up at Mom and wagged her tail, but it was a feeble flop compared to the usual thumping beat.

Mom crouched down and smiled into Poppy's troubled face. She lifted her hand and caressed Poppy's ear. Poppy leaned into her touch – ear rubs were welcome regardless of her mood.

'Do you think it's because of the puppy?' Jack asked quietly.

Mom hummed and nodded. 'I wouldn't be surprised. She was very protective of her back in the wood.' Then she turned to Poppy. 'The puppy will be all right, Pops. She's in good hands. We've just got to wait and see, but the main thing is she isn't wandering around alone out there. She could have been attacked by a fox or badger, or worst still, run over by a car or tractor.'

Poppy trembled and whined.

Mom groaned and cuddled her. 'You're a big softie, Pop.'

Jack leaned in and wrapped his arms around Poppy too, joining the group hug.

# MORNING SUNSHINE

Olde red the cockerel crowed his now-familiar croaky
warble.

Poppy lifted her head from her resting place, which
was the spot at the top of the stairs. The sun was lighting
up the sky in pastel ribbons of blue, pink and yellow. It
was going to be another bright, sunny day.

Poppy watched Carol feed the goat, hens and ducks.
Oliver and Olive trotted after her. She couldn't believe
that neither was interested in the animals' breakfast.
Had Poppy been there she'd have had her head buried
in their food bucket.

Yet, if she had a companion – the way Oliver and

Olive had each other – would she be as interested in the food? Perhaps not. Having someone to wrestle and play with was one of the best things in the world.

Her mind then wandered, wondering whether the dogs had eaten their breakfast yet. The thought of food made her stomach grumble. She was so hungry.

'Morning, Poppy,' Mom said as she climbed the stairs. 'Sleep well?'

Poppy wagged her tail and grunted.

Mom chuckled and ruffled Poppy's ears before stepping over her. 'Right then, I'll get on with breakfast.'

Poppy jumped up. 'Breakfast!' she barked, then pressed her nose against Mom's leg.

A little later, Dad appeared at the top of the stairs, his hair still bed-ruffled. He yawned and ran his hand over his stubbly chin.

Mom looked over her shoulder at him as she took a frying pan out of the cupboard.

'Can you take Poppy outside? She'll need a wee. I thought I'd cook us a full English breakfast, what do you think?'

Poppy knew what that meant and she grunted her approval. Dad's sleepy face lit up.

'Sounds good,' he said and nodded to Poppy.

'I'll make Poppy some eggs and sausages,' Mom said, reading the expression on Dad's face.

Poppy howled, 'I love holidays!' then threw her head back again and howled even louder, 'and I really love Devon!'

Dad and Poppy walked out into the garden. It was already warm, and judging by the sky it was going to get even hotter.

She saw Jack's football lying where he'd left it yesterday – in the middle of the lawn.

*What better way to start the day than with a game of football?*

She ran over to the ball and was just about to head it to Dad when Colin's truck pulled up outside the gate.

Poppy and Dad walked over to greet Colin.

'Another lovely morning,' Colin said, leaning on the gate and smiling.

Dad looked up at the sky and squinted against the sun. 'It's going to be like this for the next few days, so it said on the radio.'

Samson and Bow appeared on either side of Colin. Bow wagged her tail and walked up to the fence. She jumped up at Dad and licked his hand.

'Morning, Bow. Morning, Samson,' Dad said cheerfully, leaning over to fuss Bow.

The young collie's tail wagged even faster. Then she turned to Poppy.

Poppy barked and was pleased to see Bow return her friendly greeting.

Meanwhile, Samson watched them from beside Colin. When he caught Poppy's eye, he raised his chin but he didn't wag his tail, nor grunt or growl. Poppy's heart sank.

Colin stepped back and looked down at his younger, excitable collie.

'Bow, come on girl,' he said.

He lowered the back of his truck and Bow jumped in. Then he walked back to the gate and patted Samson's shoulder. Poppy saw the look in Samson's eyes soften and she thought for a brief moment that he was going to smile.

'We had a phone call from the vet earlier,' Colin said.

Poppy's ears twitched. She stepped closer and sat on Dad's foot.

'She's spoken to the police, but no one has reported a puppy missing.'

'So, now what?' Dad asked. Poppy could hear the concern in his voice. 'Will it stay at the surgery?'

Colin took a deep breath and pursed his lips. He shook his head slowly.

'Well, that's the problem. They've got limited space and there are already a few animals having treatment there, so they haven't got the room. We'd keep it over at the house, but it's like Carol said, her two dogs wouldn't get on with it. It wouldn't be fair on the pup or them.' He sighed and scratched his head. 'Those dogs are Carol's babies, and there's no chance they'd welcome another, even just for a day or so. They get very jealous around Carol.'

'Well…' Dad's voice trailed away. Poppy had an idea of what was on his mind. She gazed up at him, trying to will him to suggest what she hoped he was thinking.

He glanced at Poppy, then looked back at Colin.

'I could speak to Jane – see what she thinks about us keeping the puppy for now – until the owners come forward?'

*Yes!* Poppy jumped up and licked Dad's arm.

Dad stroked the top of her head and smiled.

'Seems Poppy likes that idea,' Colin said. 'If you're sure, then that would be a great help.'

'Leave it with me,' Dad said.

# PLAYTIME

Colin and Dad stood at the gate. Still deep in conversation, Colin opened the gate for Samson. The collie walked up to Poppy and sniffed her ears, cheek and paws in greeting.

'Morning to you too, Samson,' she barked. 'Do you want to play football?'

Samson looked at her and then the ball. 'OK.'

They ran to the middle of the lawn, but when he reached the football, Samson looked awkward. He jumped around then began circling it as though it was a lone sheep.

Poppy decided to make the first move. She butted

152

the ball across the grass with her nose. It rolled towards the pigs who were already pushing their noses through the fence and grunting happily.

As Poppy ran after the ball, she realised Samson wasn't following.

'Come on, Samson,' she barked, 'get the ball.'

The football stopped at the fence.

'Pigs… pigs… pigs,' the pigs grunted.

Poppy whined and did a little dance.

'Morning!' she barked, then spun around and saw Samson staring at her from the middle of the lawn.

She found his awkwardness hard to comprehend. To her, playing football and greeting others came naturally.

'Samson,' she barked, 'come here.'

She was pleased to see him run towards her. He ignored the pigs, who grunted even louder at the sight of him, and stared at Poppy and the ball instead.

Poppy jumped and barked then dived for the ball. She realised that, despite their game yesterday, he was still unsure. Yet for Poppy, the thought of playing – with Samson especially – made her happy and excited. The pigs seemed happy too. Were they cheering her on? Poppy was certain they were – urging her to go faster.

She hit the ball, making it spin across the lawn. Then, to her astonishment, Samson leapt across the grass and caught it.

The pigs cheered in a chorus of grunts, causing Samson to turn and look at them. This was the first time he'd acknowledged them. He dipped his head in a

bow and then, with the ball in his mouth, he looked at
Poppy. There it was, that sparkle in his eyes.

Poppy jumped forward. She barked and lowered her
head. With her bottom in the air and her tail wagging,
she barked at Samson again.

She heard Dad laughing, then Colin said, 'I don't
believe it. I've never seen Samson act like that, not even
when he was a pup.'

'I keep telling Jane that Poppy needs a companion.
Look how happy she is – they both are!' said Dad.

Poppy lunged towards Samson again. He dodged
past her and raced around the lawn. He looked over
his shoulder at her. Poppy knew what that look meant –
*Come and get the ball, if you can!*

Poppy ran after him, barking all the way. Meanwhile,
the pigs ran up and down the fence, grunting, 'Come
on, Poppy!'

Once she'd caught up with Samson and managed
to wrestle the ball from him, it dawned on her what the
pigs had said.

She turned to them. The pigs stared back. Samson
had no time for this and barked impatiently.

One of the pigs walked along the fence.

'Go on, Poppy,' it grunted.

Was Poppy becoming so familiar with the pigs that she was beginning to understand them? What other explanation could there be?

Suddenly, Samson lunged and knocked the ball from Poppy. She turned and ran after him.

'Just look at them go,' she heard Dad say. 'She looks even happier now she's made a new friend.'

Samson was too fast for her. He changed direction so quickly she stumbled over her own paws.

She was having the best time until she caught sight of Colin walking away.

Samson noticed her distraction. He stopped and followed her stare, then ran after Colin, barking, 'Wait, I'm coming!' He caught up with him just as he was walking through the gate. Colin leaned down and gently patted Samson's head.

'Be a good boy now. I'm taking Bow with me this morning. You stay here and look after the farm.'

Samson sat down. He watched Colin climb into the truck and drive away. For a while, he gazed at the space where the truck had been.

Poppy didn't know which field Colin and Bow were going to, but this time it wasn't opposite their cottage. She wondered just how many fields and flocks of sheep Colin and Carol had.

'Samson.'

Poppy turned and saw Carol standing outside the farmhouse. She whistled and called him again. Samson spun around and ran towards her. He sped past Poppy and the pigs, then ran through the small gate Carol held open for him.

Dad called Poppy – breakfast was ready.

She walked past the ball, no longer interested in the game. She was hungry, but her excitement for sausages and eggs had paled after seeing the hurt and confusion on Samson's face.

# PUPPY'S BACK!

The Robinsons spent the afternoon walking along Paignton's seafront. The loud noises from the arcades and the funfair frightened Poppy at first, but seeing other dogs happily walking by made her realise there was nothing to fear.

Her nose twitched at the smell of fish and chips, candy floss, shellfish and burgers. She enjoyed watching her family play a game of crazy golf and she even managed to resist the temptation to steal the ball.

Now, after such a busy day, they were back at the cottage. Evie had fallen asleep in the car so Dad carried her to bed. Jack was tired too, so tired he didn't want a game of football. Meanwhile, Poppy just wanted to relax in the sunshine. She lay out on the lawn and, with the sun warming her fur, she fell asleep.

She woke to the sound of a gate closing followed by footsteps. She looked up and saw Carol. Poppy was on her feet in an instant, all grogginess gone when she saw the little pup in Carol's arms.

Mom opened the door. Poppy heard her fussing over Pup, and their voices became muffled as Carol and Pup went inside. Poppy ran into the cottage and followed them upstairs.

Dad, Jack and Evie gathered around them. Everyone was cooing and fussing over Pup. Poppy was thrilled to see her again and relieved to see she was OK.

Everyone was smiling. Poppy could see they had all been worried for Pup and were just as happy to see her again. But the problem was Poppy couldn't see properly. Everyone was crowding around the little one.

Carol carefully placed Pup into Evie's arms. Evie's eyes were as wide and bright as her smile. Poppy could even see tears of joy.

Carol then left the Robinsons to welcome Pup into their holiday home.

Poppy walked up to Evie. Mom, Dad and Jack were still standing around them, so Poppy still couldn't see properly. She barked, 'Excuse me!'

Poppy's bark startled everyone, including Pup. The puppy wriggled so much Mom gently took her from Evie.

'Sssh. It's OK. That's just Poppy saying hello. You remember Poppy, don't you?' Mom said.

Poppy jumped up, trying to get between Mom's hands, which were shielding Pup's face.

'I can't see,' Poppy barked.

Mom turned away, saying, 'Calm down, Poppy, there's a good girl.'

Pup peered over Mom's hand and yapped, 'I've missed you, Poppy.'

'I missed you too,' Poppy barked as she jumped up again. 'Are you OK?' she moved her head from side to side. She tried squeezing her nose between Mom's hands.

'No, Poppy,' Mom said sternly, then turned her back on her and walked to the other side of the room. 'Take Poppy outside, Jon,' Mom said as she sat on the settee. Jack and Evie joined her.

Poppy would have joined them too if Dad hadn't taken hold of her collar.

'Come on, Pop. Outside,' he said, his voice gentle, so she knew she wasn't in trouble.

As Poppy was led to the stairs, she looked back over her shoulder and noticed everyone talking softly to Pup.

Once she was outside, Dad shut the door firmly behind her. Poppy looked at the closed door. She imagined Dad rushing back up the stairs to join the others.

She turned and plodded over to the grass. With a groan, she flopped down.

Through the open windows she could hear her family laughing and saying, 'Awe, did you see that?' and 'Isn't she cute?'

Although Poppy was pleased to see Pup, she couldn't help feeling left out.

*Why do I have to go outside? I want to greet Pup too.*

Poppy heard Evie laughing, and that made her feel worse. She was a part of the family too, yet at that precise moment, she felt excluded and alone. She began to understand how Samson must have felt that morning when Colin left him behind.

From across the field, she heard Colin whistle. She lifted her head and saw him herding the sheep with Samson and Bow. She watched Samson – big, proud Samson. He was sitting very still. His back was straight and he was looking at Bow. The younger collie ran around the sheep obeying Colin's instructions.

At the sight of her majestic friend, Poppy felt like crying. She knew there was nothing he wanted more than to be herding the sheep himself.

The pigs were lying out in the sun – even they were ignoring her.

Poppy grunted and flopped on to her side. She was fed up.

*Everything was fine until Pup came along.* Whenever Poppy jumped up and barked, her family usually reacted with a smile and a hug – but not today. *And why not? Because of Pup, that's why.*

The farmhouse door opened and Carol appeared on the doorstep. Poppy watched her through the grass.

Carol opened her arms and cried, 'Babies! How are we? Do you want some dinner?'

Poppy heard Oliver and Olive's barks, followed by Carol's laughter.

'How about some delicious turkey and vegetables,' she said, 'followed by frozen yoghurt?'

Then she swooped down and picked them both up, tucking one under each arm. The dogs reached up and licked her face.

*Funny,* Poppy thought, *that Carol doesn't leave either one of them out. Neither of them is cast outside on their own – unlike me.* Poppy felt very much alone.

Poppy fumed. She sighed then sneezed because of the grass tickling her nose. She could still hear her family laughing and cooing. She even heard Pup's cute little whines.

*Not one of them is missing me,* she thought. *They've forgotten I'm even here.*

Poppy whined. For the first time in her life, she felt completely ignored and as though her place in the Robinson family was threatened. Would they replace her with Pup? The little one was cuter than her, all puppies were.

Then she heard Mom say, 'Right, let's get a photo.'

A family holiday tradition – as Dad called it.

'Yes, a holiday tradition – without me,' Poppy grumbled. 'I wish I'd never found Pup now.'

Poppy felt even worse, knowing that what she was thinking was not a nice thing at all.

# THE BYSTANDER

It had been a strange evening and one Poppy hadn't enjoyed.

Fearing she'd get into trouble, Poppy had kept a distance from her family and Pup, choosing to lie on the top of the stairs and look out of the window instead.

She did as she was told. When Dad went outside, she followed. When they played with Pup, she lay down and ignored them. There was no point in joining the game, no matter how much she'd have loved to. She knew she'd only get into trouble.

But when a member of her family did come over, she enjoyed the fuss, the tickles on her tummy, the chin rubs and the ear ruffles. It was just a shame it didn't last long enough.

Olde Red croaked his usual morning call, welcoming another hot and sunny day.

Poppy stretched and padded down the stairs, following Dad outside. She tried not to feel annoyed and jealous. But it was difficult. Near impossible. She couldn't help being envious, knowing where Pup had spent the night.

Poppy growled and grumbled to herself as she plodded on to the lawn. She had never been allowed to sleep in Mom and Dad's room, not in all her four years. But here was the little pup – at what? Three or four months old? – sleeping beside their bed. It wasn't fair!

She sniffed the ground, smelling where the rabbits had been. She heard Colin's whistle and knew instantly where it came from.

She looked across at the field and saw Samson. He looked sad and lonely as he watched Colin and Bow at work. Her heart ached to see him like this. He was just like her – a bystander.

*What's wrong with hoomans at times?* Poppy cussed. *Don't they think we dogs have feelings too?*

Colin whistled, but Bow hesitated. Poppy noticed the

young collie look at Samson, then take a step towards him. Colin whistled again. Samson barked, and even from where Poppy was standing, his meaning was loud and clear: *Go on. Don't stop!*

Bow circled the sheep, keeping her body low to the ground. Poppy had excellent eyesight as well as a keen sense of hearing. She noticed Bow's hesitation and how she kept glancing back at Samson.

*Is Samson making her nervous?* Poppy wouldn't have been surprised if he was. She remembered how he had made her feel when she first met him.

Colin walked over to his trusted old collie. He stood beside him and patted him on the head. Poppy was surprised to see Samson didn't respond. Then again, she didn't blame him.

Colin called out, 'Come by.' Bow stood up. She moved a couple of steps, then paused. She looked at Samson again.

*Is she waiting for his approval?* Poppy had a feeling she was.

Samson barked, 'Don't dither. Go!'

Bow sprang into action.

Once a portion of the flock was herded into the next field, Colin walked over to Bow. Bow basked in the praise their master lavished upon her. Meanwhile, Samson looked on.

Poppy growled. She growled louder as her anger grew. *Poor Samson.*

Bow approached the older and wiser collie. Poppy noticed how slowly she moved: cautious and submissive. Yet, Samson ignored her. He sat looking out at the sheep. Bow took another hesitant step towards him, her head and tail held low.

Colin called Samson. Instantly the collie went to work. He ran around the remaining sheep, herding them closely together. His movements were steady and quick. His attention was focused only on the sheep and Colin.

Poppy was impressed. *Bow could learn a lot from him. There isn't another collie around who can control sheep as well as Samson. Bow has a good teacher.*

Colin called his younger collie to his side. She settled at his feet and watched Samson – the master – at work.

Poppy wondered, perhaps Samson wasn't being replaced? From what she could see, Colin and Samson were *teaching* the young collie.

# A MISUNDERSTANDING

Dad appeared beside Poppy. She'd been so engrossed with Colin and his dogs that she hadn't heard him approach. He stood next to her and buried his hands in his pockets. He watched Colin and his collies at work.

'Wishing you were out there too, Pop?' he said.

Poppy refused to acknowledge Dad. She was still too cross with the hoomans; and besides, she wanted to give Dad a taste of his own medicine.

They watched in silence until a door could be heard opening and closing. Poppy turned to the sound of footsteps running over gravel.

'Dad! What are you doing? Breakfast will be ready soon,' Jack shouted as he ran towards them in his Kentley Town FC pyjamas.

Poppy wagged her tail. She couldn't be annoyed with her brother, even though he'd been playing with Pup too – and for far too long, in her opinion.

As he came over, she reached towards him and licked the back of his hand.

'Hey, Poppy.' Jack stroked the top of her head.

'Bow's doing a good job, don't you think?' Dad said, still watching Colin and his collies at work.

Jack looked at the sheep being herded across the field. 'I wonder how long it takes to train a dog to do that,' he said.

'Oooh… a while, I should think.'

'Do you think Poppy could do it?'

Dad chuckled – much to Poppy's displeasure.

*What's funny?* she grumbled. *I could round up sheep if Samson showed me how.* Yet she knew it would take a long time and much patience to become anywhere near as good as Samson and Bow.

'They're training Bow to be another sheepdog,' Dad said. 'She's going to be Samson's companion. Colin's planning to buy more sheep, that's why Samson's getting some help.'

Poppy looked up at him. Her mood brightened. *So Samson isn't being replaced after all! He isn't going to be sent away. His place on the farm isn't threatened.* It was as she'd just thought: Bow was being trained to help, *not* take over.

'Colin will have his hands full controlling two dogs and all those sheep,' Jack said, his eyes still on the farmer.

'That won't be a problem for Colin. The difficulty will be getting Samson to accept the younger collie.'

'Samson's a bit of a grump isn't he?' Jack said as he absently reached out to Poppy. 'I remember what he was like with Poppy when she ran into him at the beach.'

Dad smiled and shook his head.

'It'll do him good,' he said, 'to have a dog companion. Carol and Colin have said that Samson isn't very good with other dogs – except Pop, that is.' He glanced over at Poppy while Jack gently stroked the silky fur around her ears. 'Samson's warmed to our Poppy, hasn't he?'

Poppy felt comforted. Her black mood was lifting.

'Apparently, Samson needs to lighten up. He needs to learn that life is for enjoying and not just work. The old boy needs a friend.'

Jack nodded. 'It's like playing football. It's better in a team than playing alone.'

Poppy noticed Dad staring at her. He seemed deep in thought, but she had no idea why. Then he smiled and patted Jack's shoulder.

'You're right, Jack,' he said. 'Come on now. Get yourself washed and dressed.'

As Jack ran back inside, Dad walked over to the table where his mug of coffee was getting cold.

Poppy decided to have a mooch around the garden. She snorted the grass. Samson's scent still lingered from their game yesterday. She couldn't wait to see him again and tell him what she'd just heard.

The pigs grunted. Poppy looked up and saw them watching her. They fidgeted as she walked over to them, their grunts getting louder and faster.

'Pigs… pigs… Poppy.'

Poppy stood in front of them and barked. 'Did you just say my name?'

The pigs looked up at her. They grunted, 'Poppy.'

She danced on the spot, happy to know she'd made new friends, and that slowly she was beginning to understand the pigs' language.

'And what are your names?' she growled.

'Pigs… pigs… pigs.'

She sighed, then decided to do what the pigs seemed to enjoy. She ran along the fence – up and down, backwards and forwards.

Whilst she ran, the pigs trotted after her, grunting as they went. Poppy was enjoying herself, but after a while she grew tired.

'I'm going to have a lie down. See you later,' she barked. The pigs stood together and watched her walk away.

170

Poppy flopped down on the lawn and groaned. She closed her eyes, but only briefly because she heard the chair creaking as Dad stood up.

Her eyelids felt heavy but she forced them open, curious to know what Dad was up to. He walked towards her. He was smiling and carrying something in his hand. She raised her head for a better view.

On closer inspection, she realised it was one of her favourite toys – a pair of Dad's old socks tied together. As Dad drew closer, Poppy's tail smacked against the grass.

*A game? Now that's more like it.*

Dad threw the socks to her and this time she caught them. *Yes! Now that doesn't happen every day.*

She shook her head, feeling the socks swaying and flapping. She sidestepped Dad, urging him to try and take them back.

'Go on,' she growled, her tail swinging and paws dancing and trotting on the spot.

Dad reached out. 'Come here,' he said, smiling.

But the moment he stepped forward, Poppy ran towards the fence. The pigs grunted happily seeing their friend return.

Poppy stopped and turned around. Dad was watching her, still smiling.

'Come here, then,' he said. He crouched down and held his hand out. 'Come on, fetch. Retrieve!' Now he was laughing.

Poppy's tail beat briskly from side to side, making her bottom wiggle too.

'Retrieve. Come on!'

Dad said this to her all the time. She had no idea what he meant, but what she did know was that he always ended up chasing her around the garden.

Dad took a step forward and reached his hand out.

Poppy closed her jaws tighter around the socks. As he took another step, she jumped to the side.

'Poppy, you're a retriever, you should retrieve!'

She replied with a playful growl-howl.

Dad ran towards her. She turned tail and raced to the far side of the lawn. He could never keep up with her. When he reached her, she dodged past, growling happily. She ran into the middle of the lawn, the socks still in her mouth, and waited for him to chase her again.

'Breakfast's ready,' Evie called from the doorway.

The smell of sausages and eggs drifted through the open windows. Poppy wanted to charge inside and race up the stairs, then bury her head in her food bowl – but she didn't.

Things were different now Pup was here. So she decided to stay outside, despite her rumbling stomach.

# A NEW GAME

Poppy lay on the grass chewing Dad's old socks. She gripped the soggy cloth with her back teeth and gnawed. Her paws held them firmly in place and she was happily losing herself in this game of chomping and pulling, when Dad walked outside carrying a plate of toast.

He settled down at the garden table and was quickly joined by Jack. They both sat finishing their breakfast whilst watching Poppy.

The smell of hot buttered toast made Poppy's mouth water. She was about to join them in the hope for a piece, but then she remembered Pup. With the little one around, nothing was safe.

Poppy was having so much fun playing with the old socks. She glanced around. Pup was nowhere to be seen. *Good.*

The way things were, she had to protect what was hers.

So, for a start, she'd make sure the socks remained *her* socks and not Pup's. She tightened her grip as she chewed. She shook her head and growled. With the socks clasped between her paws, she closed her eyes and munched again on the soggy cloth.

Dad and Jack were laughing. She didn't take much notice until something fell against her. Poppy opened her eyes and saw Pup trying to steal her socks.

*How rude.*

Pup pushed her nose against Poppy's and growled. 'Can I play?'

Poppy jumped up. 'No,' she growled back.

She turned her back on Pup and carried on gnawing at the socks, only this time with more conviction. Pup needed to know these were hers and no one else's. But Pup tumbled into her again and began chewing her ear.

'Get off,' Poppy growled.

Pup ignored her. She tugged and pulled.

'I said get off!' Poppy tried pulling her head away.

Pup wouldn't give in. She let go of Poppy's ear but grabbed the socks instead.

'Mine.' Poppy growled and pulled – but Pup wouldn't let go. 'Get off,' she growled again.

With her bottom in the air and shoulders down, she pulled back – this time with more force. The socks, and Pup, were lifted off the floor.

Pup shook her head and growled, although it sounded more like a purr to Poppy. Her chubby legs swung in the air from side to side like the pendulum of an old grandfather clock. Poppy loosened her grip so the little one could safely land back on the grass. Pup dug her paws into the ground and pulled on the socks with all her might.

They looked into each other's eyes. Neither was going to back down.

As Poppy growled, so did Pup. As Poppy pulled and tugged, so did Pup. When Poppy shook her head… so did Pup.

*She's enjoying this,* Poppy realised with surprise. Pup was thrashing her head from side to side, yanking and tugging at the socks.

Poppy was a lot stronger than Pup, but the little one's determination took her by surprise, causing her to lose her grip. She stood back, licking her lips, as the socks were pulled from her grasp.

Pup trotted away, the prize held firmly in her mouth. She pulled her fluffy head back, trying to keep them from trailing on the floor. As she struggled, Poppy seized her chance and lunged for the socks – *her* socks.

'Mine,' Poppy growled, dragging them away from Pup.

But her success was short-lived. Pup was not going to be beaten. The little one barked and leapt forward, seizing the other end of the socks in her mouth once again. She pulled. Poppy pulled too.

'Mine,' Pup growled.

Poppy stumbled. She caught the mischievous glint in the Pup's eye. *She thinks this is a game!* Pup tugged again.

Poppy pulled back. Their eyes locked onto each other. They growled softly. Pup suddenly thrashed her head as she desperately tried to win the game. As Poppy took a step back, Pup – still refusing to let go – was dragged along the lawn. Poppy grunted. *This isn't so bad.* Her tail wagged faster. Her heartbeat quickened. Then, Poppy made a shocking discovery – she was enjoying the game too.

They heaved and pulled, skidded and thrashed. Playing tug-of-war with Pup was more fun than chewing the socks alone.

Just as she was enjoying this new game, an irresistible smell tickled Poppy's nose. Glancing sideways, she saw Mom holding a bowl of sausages and eggs out to her.

Poppy leapt up and devoured the delicious breakfast in no time. She licked the empty bowl clean, then just for good measure, licked it again.

Mom ruffled Poppy's ears. 'Did you enjoy that?' she said, laughing.

Poppy looked up at her. She licked her lips then belched. 'Yes, thank you.'

Now her tummy was full, Poppy was even happier. She turned back to the socks and pounced. Pup followed and took hold of the other end.

Poppy's mood brightened further when Evie joined them and sat beside Poppy with a brush in her hand. Poppy loved being groomed.

She let go of the socks, sending Pup tumbling backwards. She rolled on to her back, hoping to be brushed on her tummy first. She pulled her head back, her jowls falling from her teeth. She bent her front paws against her chest and sighed, feeling the long soft strokes of the brush.

'This is nice,' she groaned and closed her eyes.

Pup was still moving about. *Oh no…*

Opening one eye, she saw the puppy lolloping towards her. Poppy sighed. She grumbled. She groaned, knowing that the delightful grooming session was about to end.

Poppy braced herself, ready for the little one's attack, but Dad appeared – just in the nick of time. He whisked Pup up in his arms and sat on the grass beside Poppy and Evie.

Pup happily chewed Dad's fingers. Poppy was glad of the distraction for her.

'Dad,' Evie said, whilst brushing the grass out of Poppy's fur, 'what shall we call her?'

'How about Socks?' Dad said. 'She seems to like them.'

Evie chuckled. 'Or,' she said in a long, drawn-out voice, 'we could call her Lady, after Lady and the Tramp.'

Dad suddenly gasped and drew his hand away, shaking his fingers. 'We could, but she's no lady. I think Shark would suit her better.'

'How about we don't give her a name at all?' Mom said.

Mom was sitting at the table with Jack. She was smiling and holding up her camera.

Dad and Evie looked up.

'I think it's a bad idea to give her a name,' Mom continued. 'She isn't our dog. If we get too attached, it'll be hard saying goodbye when her owners come for her.'

Dad nodded. 'Your mom's right, Evie.'

Evie stopped brushing.

Poppy sighed, realising her grooming session was over. She stood up, had a quick shake, making her jowls slap, then licked Evie's hand before sitting back down.

Even though Evie looked sad, Poppy was happy. Mom had said they were only keeping Pup for a short while, which meant Poppy would have her family all to herself again soon.

Poppy heard Colin's truck making its way down the country lane long before she saw it. She stood and watched him drive past. He blasted his horn and waved as he went by.

Samson sat in the back with Bow. The young collie looked up at him, but he'd turned his back on her and, Poppy guessed, had no intention of turning around.

Poppy needed to see Samson and tell him what Dad had said. The sooner he knew that Bow wasn't replacing him, the better. Then, perhaps Bow and Samson would be a lot happier and could maybe even become friends.

# SEA, SAND, SUNSHINE... AND FOOTBALL!

Poppy and Pup were engrossed in another game of tug-of-war. Meanwhile, Mom and Dad loaded the car with towels and bags.

'Are you sure you don't mind staying here?' Dad said to Mom.

Mom shut the back door then turned to Dad. 'Yes. Evie and I will be fine.'

Poppy was curious and quickly lost interest in the game. She trotted over to Mom and gently pushed her nose into her hand.

Jack charged out of the house, bouncing his football, while Evie rushed up to Pup and gently picked her up.

'Can we take the puppy to the beach another day?' Jack said as he opened the back door.

There was the magic word – Beach!

Thoughts of sand, ice cream, ball games and ice cream came to Poppy's mind. She whined. She couldn't help it, she was too excited. But then she remembered what the others had just said.

*Mom, Evie and Pup are staying behind.*

Poppy sat down and whined. Sometimes, she didn't understand her own feelings. She loved the thought of having Dad and Jack to herself. But the idea of Mom and Evie staying behind was not so good. And the fact that Pup was staying away too made her feel sad. Then, she remembered her last trip to the beach. She groaned, remembering the bad-tempered Yorkshire terrier and it's even angrier owner.

Poppy wasn't so sure that a visit to the beach was a good idea after all, but everyone was talking, so she decided to listen.

'The puppy needs her vaccinations before she can go anywhere,' Mom was saying, 'She needs protection against serious dog illnesses like distemper.'

'So she's safe here?' Jack asked.

'Yes. We'll keep her around the cottage and in the garden,' Mom said.

Dad opened the back door and said, 'It's better to be safe than sorry, Jack. Now get yourself in. I'll buy you an ice cream when we get to the beach.'

Jack climbed into the car.

'Ice cream!' Poppy barked, then dived in after him.

Dad pulled up at the Sand Dunes car park. Poppy peered through the window. She was looking for the Yorkshire terrier. He may have been small, but he was scary.

Dad opened the back door and Poppy jumped out on to the sand. She smelt the fresh, salty sea air.

A seagull glided past. It opened its yellow beak and made the most awful noise. Poppy shrank back. She hated the sound of seagulls. She watched it sail through the air towards the refreshment hut. She knew what the bird wanted, because she wanted the same. The mouth-watering smell of chips and burgers tickled her nose. She licked her lips. OK, so it wasn't long since her breakfast, but that didn't mean she wasn't interested in the food, especially the sort that sizzled and spat as it cooked.

Jack climbed out of the car, his football tucked under his arm.

'Come on, Pops,' he said.

Poppy ran with Jack and Dad towards a clearing on the beach. She forgot about the terrier as she raced backwards and forwards after the football. Dad dribbled the ball around her. Jack sped past. He took the ball from Dad and launched it into the air.

Poppy jumped up, her eyes fixed on the ball.

'I've got it! I've got it!' she barked happily.

As it came down, her grin faded. That ball was hers. She was determined to catch it.

Dad ran towards her. Poppy's eyes moved back to the ball. It was falling, closer and closer…

'It's mine!' she barked, 'I've got it.'

She jumped up. She opened her mouth, ready to catch the ball. It was moving fast and then… it landed on the tip of her nose and bounced in the opposite direction.

Poppy shook her head and sneezed. She was caught off guard, but not for long. She raced after it, intent on only one thing – reaching the ball first.

The chase was on…

Dad was close behind and gaining every second. She ran faster, easily leaving Dad behind. Swooping down, she seized the ball with her teeth.

*Yes!*

Poppy lifted her head triumphantly, the ball firmly held in place.

She trotted up and down the beach, holding the ball aloft like a trophy.

'Look at me,' she grunted, 'look what I've got.'

This was turning out to be a much better day than her last visit to the beach.

Dad and Jack caught up with her. Both were grinning, their hands held high, waiting to make their move.

Poppy wagged her tail, waiting for them to try and take the ball off her, but Dad suddenly looked past her. He stood up straight and smiled.

'Morning, Flo,' he said.

Poppy turned and came face to face with Samson.

The shock of seeing him caught her off guard. Jack noticed this and quickly took the ball.

Poppy glanced at Jack, watching him race away with the football. But Poppy had lost all interest in their game.

'Hello, Samson,' she barked and wagged her tail.

The collie walked up to her and gently rubbed his nose against hers.

*Could this morning get any better?*

Samson jumped back, then turned and ran off.

Poppy was confused. *What's wrong with him?* She tilted her head left and right.

Samson looked over his shoulder and barked, 'Come on, Poppy.'

She didn't need to be asked twice.

# RUNNING LIKE A WOODVILLE

Poppy and Samson ran and ran. She had no idea how far they'd gone, but it felt like miles.

Now she was tired. She thought her legs would buckle beneath her. Eventually, she had no option but to stop. Samson turned and walked back towards her.

*He's not even panting!* she thought, as her tongue hung from the side of her mouth. She took heavy, rasping breaths.

'Shall we head back?' Samson barked. Poppy noticed the glint of amusement in his eyes.

She nodded because she didn't have the energy to bark. She needed a drink and hoped Dad would have her water ready.

While walking back to the others, Poppy's heart returned to its steady rhythm and she finally caught her breath.

As she'd hoped, there was a bottle of water ready. Poppy and Samson drank, Dad holding it for them. Afterwards, they lay on the sand and had a rest.

Poppy seized this moment to tell him what she'd discovered about Bow.

Samson listened.

'So Bow isn't replacing you, Samson,' she whined and was pleased to see him nodding slowly, listening to everything she said. 'I've seen the way she looks at you,' Poppy continued. 'She looks up to you. She wants your approval. To be honest, you do put others on edge sometimes.'

Samson tilted his head.

'Do I?' he barked.

'When I first met you, you made me really nervous. You need to have more fun. Life's for enjoying too.'

Samson nodded. 'I've heard Colin say the same. So that's why Flo's started taking me to the beach? I thought it was to get me out of the way.'

Poppy dipped her head. 'I know.'

Samson stood up and, lifting his paw, he tapped her on the shoulder. 'Thank you, Poppy.'

Suddenly, Jack's ball flew past them. Poppy jumped up.

'Come on, Samson,' she barked.

They chased the ball. Poppy couldn't believe that Samson, of all dogs, was racing along beside her. Just a few days ago, she'd never have thought they'd become good friends. How funny and unexpected life could be sometimes.

Dad, Jack and Flo eventually caught up. They kicked the ball between them. Poppy and Samson occasionally managed to intercept it and carry it away.

Poppy noticed how Flo looked at Samson. Her rosy cheeks, sparkling eyes and big smile left Poppy in no doubt that she was surprised and happy to see Samson having so much fun.

Flo took the ball from Jack. She kicked it towards Dad but it flew past him. They all ran after it. Poppy focused on the ball. Samson ran beside her. They were neck and neck. She could hear the others behind them, their footsteps splashing in the water.

Her paws were wet. The sand felt smoother, firmer and damp. Her claws were sinking. She looked down. To her horror, she saw water rushing backwards and forwards between her paws. To and fro. This made her head feel very strange. Then it dawned on her.

She wasn't just standing *in water* – she was *knee-deep* in the sea itself!

# POPPY THE BRAVE

Poppy froze. She stared at the water. Her claws were sinking. The feathering on her legs stuck to her skin. Her heart was racing and panic was taking over.

'Poppy? What's the matter?' Samson barked.

She glanced at him then looked to the sky. She couldn't look at the water anymore. It was making her head feel funny. Her heart was racing. She hated the sensation of the waves whooshing backwards and forwards. She was certain that at any moment she would fall. She whined, trying to concentrate on the seagulls flying overhead.

Then she heard Samson step closer.

'Poppy?'

She whined and forced herself to look at him.

'Get me out, Samson. I don't like it,' she said.

Meanwhile, Dad, Jack and Flo called out to Poppy and Samson. Jack was in the sea up to his waist although he didn't seem to mind.

'Poppy's never gone out this far on her own,' Jack said to Flo.

'A retriever that doesn't like water? Really?' Flo laughed.

Dad leaned forward, his hands on his knees, and called, 'Poppy.'

But she couldn't move. Her legs were rigid, while her claws were sinking further into the wet sand.

She looked at Dad and howled, 'Get me out!'

Dad smiled. He took hold of her collar and tried pulling her farther into the sea. She pulled back against him.

*No! Wrong way. I want to get out not go deeper.* She wanted to bark, but her terror stopped her.

Eventually, Dad gave up. He sighed and picked her up.

*This is so embarrassing – and in front of Samson too.*

She stared ahead. She refused to look at Samson. Others were watching. Some were laughing. It was too much.

The moment they were on dry land, Poppy wriggled to be free.

Dad let her go and she shook herself violently, shaking the salty water from her coat.

'Poppy, I had no idea you didn't like water,' Flo said.

Samson gently bumped Poppy's nose with his muzzle.

'Before you were in the sea, you were enjoying the game, weren't you?' he whined.

Poppy nodded. Gradually, her heartbeat steadied and her trembles eased.

Samson sat in front of her.

'But, you were already knee-deep in the water before you realised you were in the sea.'

Poppy looked at him. *What's your point, Samson?* she wondered.

'Nothing bad happened, did it?' he growled.

She thought about it for a moment then shook her head.

'We were having fun,' he growled.

Poppy thought about their game – feeling the sea breeze against her fur, the thrill of the chase, even the cool water splashing over her and cooling her down. Actually, it had felt quite nice.

Meanwhile, the others were heading back into the sea. They were laughing and throwing the ball at each other.

Samson stood up.

'Come on,' he growled, 'we'll go back in together.'

He was panting softly, his wet nose twitching and shining in the sunlight – he looked happy.

'Come on, give it another try,' he coaxed. 'We'll just get our paws wet. We won't go any deeper if you don't want to.' He took a step back and then looked at the others.

Poppy heard them laughing. They seemed to be having fun.

She remembered the times she'd watched Samson on the field with Colin and Bow. The times he'd sat away from them, not joining in, ignoring them. She'd seen how detached he looked and now she was beginning to feel the same way. Everyone else was having fun. No one was in danger and no one seemed scared.

The ball bounced along the waves. Jack swooped down and picked it up, the water rolling and splashing down his arms. He couldn't stop laughing.

'Poppy,' Samson disturbed her thoughts, 'come on.'

He walked a few paces then turned and stopped.

'It's more fun if you join in. Just give it another try. If you don't like it then I promise we'll stay on the sand.'

She noticed the way he looked at her. At that moment she realised how much she trusted him. She also knew that Dad and Jack would never let anything bad happen to her.

*Perhaps it won't hurt just to give it another try?* If she didn't then she knew she'd regret it.

They walked into the sea together. Dad, Jack and Flo stopped playing catch and watched them approach.

'Come on, Poppy,' Dad said. He was smiling.

She took a cautious step into the water; Samson was by her side.

'OK?' he growled.

Poppy grunted. She took another step, then another.

'Poppy!' Jack shouted, waving his arms in the air.

She looked up and barked.

Samson barked too, 'Shall we try a little deeper?'

She followed him steadily, going deeper still.

*Has anything bad happened? No,* she concluded, *And it does feel nice.*

Poppy barked again and again. Samson spun around and they ran through the waves together. She leapt over the water, this time loving the feel of it splashing against her legs, her body and her face.

Dad stood a little further ahead. As long as she didn't venture too far, she'd be all right. If she stayed where she was, surrounded by her family and new friends, Poppy was safe.

A wave rolled towards them and Poppy jumped. She cleared it and barked in celebration. Wave upon wave followed. They'd run. They'd jump. They'd clear the waves and then she saw it. A large wave rolling towards them. It swelled bigger and bigger as it travelled to the shore. Her heart raced. *I can clear this. I'll show everyone just how agile I can be.* But then she stumbled.

Down she went, tumbling into the sea beneath the

191

waves. She whimpered and trembled then decided to seize the panic. *Stay calm. I can do this.* She pushed her head up out of the water. The waves rocked her body gently as the water lapped over her back.

*What just happened? Why am I so clumsy?*

As she lay on her stomach, the water washing over her, she looked across at Samson. He was watching her, and then suddenly he fell into the water too.

Poppy was confused.

*What is he doing? Is Samson OK?*

He rolled on to his back, his legs kicking and thrashing, sending water splashing everywhere.

Poppy tilted her head.

He rolled on to his stomach. His face was dripping wet. Grains of wet sand clung to his fur. He opened his mouth and barked.

For a moment, they lay on their stomachs, two soaking wet dogs both being rocked by the gentle surge of the sea.

Samson barked again – a loud, high-pitched, excited bark. He jumped up, then fell back down. He rolled over and over in the water.

That looked like a lot of fun. Poppy wanted to join in – so she did.

# CHANGES

That evening, Poppy lay by the fireplace dreaming about the sea. The rolling waves. The splashing and jumping. The sun on her face.

She opened one eye at the sound of the front door opening then closing again. She lifted her head, hearing footsteps climbing the stairs. She knew who it was. Mom's flowery perfume had tickled her nose the moment she had walked into the cottage.

'Any news?' Dad asked as Mom sat down.

Mom shook her head, 'Carol says if no one comes forward soon, they'll have to think about rehoming her.'

194

Poppy knew who they were talking about. She looked across the room to where Jack and Pup were playing. The little one was growling and wriggling on her back as Jack tickled her tum. Meanwhile, Evie was curled up on the settee, cuddling and chatting to Buttercup – Poppy still couldn't believe how she could have mistaken Buttercup for a real puppy. Especially when she watched how wriggly and fidgety Pup was. And as for that cute, puppy voice of hers…

'Can we keep her, Mom?' Jack asked, tearing his eyes away from Pup for a moment.

'Don't stop,' Pup squeak-barked.

Mom looked from Pup to Poppy. She seemed troubled. Poppy noticed she was chewing the inside of her cheek. That was always a sign something was on her mind.

Pup squeak-barked again. Jack whisked her up in his arms and buried his nose in her fluffy fur, then blew a raspberry on her plump, velvety tummy.

Despite her feelings of pity towards Pup for having to stay home the day before – and even though she was being irresistibly cute tonight – Poppy was annoyed at how much attention she was getting. Poppy looked around at everyone, hoping to catch someone's eye. Dad was making a coffee. Mom was sitting in the armchair looking thoughtful. Evie was playing with Buttercup, and Jack only had eyes for Pup.

*Won't anyone pay me some attention too?* Poppy lifted her head, stretched her neck and then crossed her paws. She was wide awake now.

She sighed. No reaction. She grunted. Nothing. She whined. Still nothing, but then…

Mom looked at her. Poppy's heart rose. She was about to wag her tail when Pup yapped at Jack, diverting Mom's gaze again.

Poppy groaned. *Typical.*

Pup wriggled on her back and chewed her paw. Mom laughed. Jack laughed. Dad and Evie looked to see what was so funny, then they laughed too.

Poppy grumbled to herself. *All those eyes on Pup – it isn't fair.* She lowered her chin on to her paws and sighed. *I might as well go outside, no one will notice.*

'Mom? Can we keep her?' Evie said, repeating the question Jack had asked earlier.

Mom sighed.

Poppy dreaded her answer. If Pup came to live with them, then every evening would be like this and Poppy didn't fancy that.

Today had been fun, one of the happiest she'd ever had – and Pup had stayed at home. Had the puppy been there, Poppy guessed she'd have spent the whole time lying on the beach, watching everyone fussing over Pup and ignoring her – and that included Samson. Poppy growled at the thought.

She didn't realise she'd growled out loud until Mom looked at her.

Mom said, 'I don't think keeping the puppy would be a good idea. It's not fair on Poppy.'

Evie cast Buttercup aside and sat on the floor beside

Poppy. She kissed the top of her head. Poppy grunted with pleasure.

'Poppy loves the puppy,' Evie said.

Poppy glared. *I don't think so,* she grumbled.

Mom hummed, making Poppy turn and look at her. She was pleased to see she had her attention at last. But Mom looked troubled.

'I don't know…' her voice trailed away.

'But Mom,' Evie said, her voice one long-drawn-out whine. 'Please? Poppy will be all right.' She crawled over to Jack and Pup.

'Poppy's used to getting all our attention. Having a playmate is very different from having another dog living with us.'

Poppy scowled as Pup's tail thumped against the floor, her soft growls making the children giggle.

Poppy had seen enough. She stood up and walked downstairs. The front door was closed so she barked, as loud as she could, 'Someone open the door, please!'

When no one responded, she barked again. She could hear everyone laughing at Pup, followed by more of her squeak-barks, which made them laugh even harder. Poppy's mood went from bad to worse. She needed to get outside.

'Someone. Open. The. Door. Please!'

Finally, Dad walked downstairs.

'All right, all right, I'm coming,' he said, then reached over and opened the door.

Poppy walked outside and heard the door close

behind her. She turned around. Dad hadn't followed. She was alone.

Poppy plodded towards the lawn. It was still light, the sun had not yet set, but the intense heat was now replaced with a temperature Poppy found more comfortable.

'Pigs… pigs… Poppy!'

Poppy looked up to see the pigs watching her.

She barked softly, returning their greeting. It was nice to hear them say her name. Pity she didn't know theirs yet. She walked over to them. Maybe a chat with her new friends would cheer her up?

'Good evening,' she growled and stood in front of them. 'What are your names?'

The pigs jostled each other while pushing their snouts through the fence.

'Poppy,' they grunted.

'No way! Really?' she barked, wagging her tail.

'Poppy… Poppy… Poppy.'

Poppy sighed. *Oh, I see…*

Feeling deflated, she turned and walked away. The pigs continued to grunt her name.

She sighed.

*Why is everything so complicated? Why can't I just be happy with Pup? Why can't I like her?*

Poppy felt sorry for Pup, that much was true, but the thought of a puppy sharing her home, her toys and her family was too much.

She wished Samson was here. *He'd understand. He knows what it feels like to be left out, unwanted, replaced. Yet, Samson was mistaken, he wasn't being replaced after all – unlike me.*

Poppy whined. She felt an ache of sadness in her chest. *Why can't everything stay the same? Why do things have to change?*

She remembered how she had felt when she found Pup in the wood. Poppy had feared for the puppy's safety and was relieved when Samson had called for help. But now all she could think about was the look on Jack and Evie's face when they played with Pup, and how happy she made everyone feel.

Poppy had been so wrapped up in her thoughts that she hadn't realised she was wandering towards the trees.

It didn't feel so frightening in there now she knew there were no wild dogs on the prowl. She heard the rapid sound of paws, and bushes rustling. Looking up, she saw two rabbits disappearing into a wall of ferns. She sighed and looked away. The thought of chasing them didn't appeal to her today.

A squirrel ran out in front of her. Poppy stopped and stared, noticing the squirrel's nose and whiskers twitching as it stood looking at her. For a few seconds neither moved, until the squirrel, realising Poppy was no threat, scampered up a nearby tree.

Poppy sauntered on. She wasn't a bit interested in rabbits or squirrels.

Her mind was a jumble of thoughts. She loved her life the way it was, she didn't want anything to change, especially with a new addition to the family. The Robinsons' lavished love and attention on her, and Poppy couldn't have been happier. But Pup would change all that. She was cuter and funnier than Poppy, there was no point denying it. Poppy was no fool, she could see how much her family loved the puppy.

*Of course, they want to keep her. But, what about Pup's own family? Where did she come from? She said she liked her home, her cosy bed, and if she hadn't wandered off, she'd still be happy there.*

Poppy decided she needed to investigate. She needed to find out exactly where Pup came from.

*Maybe there is another farm or cottage nearby?*

*Strange that they haven't reported their puppy missing, but then again, perhaps they have and the news just hasn't reached the vet and the police yet?* Poppy hoped so because she hated the thought of the little one being sent to a rescue centre with other unwanted and abandoned dogs.

'Poppy!'

Dad's voice echoed around the wood, followed by his loud, sharp whistle.

'Poppy! Dinner!'

She turned around and trundled back through the wood and towards the cottage. Even though Dad had said another magic word – dinner – she was in no rush. Poppy didn't feel that hungry.

# IT WASN'T MY FAULT

'What have you been up to, eh?' Dad said as Poppy passed him on the doorstep.

He closed the door after her and she plodded up the stairs. She could smell the tripe and vegetables from the front door. She could also hear Pup slapping and slurping as she ate. Poppy guessed the puppy was nearly finished because she could hear the bowl skidding across the floor.

Even though she didn't feel that hungry, she couldn't help drooling at the delicious smell. She loved tripe.

Poppy sat at Dad's feet and waited patiently. Dad smiled and lowered the bowl to the floor.

Meanwhile, Pup stood licking her lips. She looked at Poppy's food bowl, her nose twitching at the smell of tripe. Poppy saw her out of the corner of her eye, so she swooped down and buried her face in her dinner before the little one beat her to it.

She could feel Pup's eyes on her – watching her every move. Meanwhile, Mom, Jack and Evie had settled on the settee while Dad finished his chores in the kitchen.

Poppy grunted. She ate as quickly as she could. She could see Pup's little black nose edging nearer. Poppy gobbled down her food. She gulped, she grunted, she coughed and she chomped.

'Don't be a pig, Poppy,' Dad said, glancing down at her as he stood at the sink, his hands buried in washing up bubbles. 'You'll make yourself sick.'

But that little face kept edging closer. Poppy swallowed a large piece of carrot and it stuck in her throat. She lifted her head and grunted then coughed. With the carrot now back on its way to her stomach, she turned her attention back to her dinner, but now there was a little golden head with big fluffy ears chomping on her tripe and vegetables.

'Off!' Poppy barked and snarled. She snapped at Pup, her teeth brushing the little one's ear. She had no intention of hurting her, just scaring her a little.

It worked. Pup backed away, cowering. Dad bent down and lifted her into his arms.

Hearing Poppy telling Pup off, Mom rushed into the kitchen.

'What's going on?' she asked, then looked at Poppy who was now quickly finishing her dinner while Pup looked at her from the safety of Dad's arms.

'This little one got a bit too close to Poppy, that's all,' Dad said, trying to lighten the mood with a little laugh.

'I thought you were keeping an eye on them,' Mom said. Poppy could tell by the tone of her voice that she was cross.

'Yes, I was, and washing up. I haven't got eyes in the back of my head.'

'She could have bitten her,' Mom's voice grew louder, 'I told you we should have fed them at different times.'

'Oh, Poppy's all right,' Dad said and lowered Pup to the ground. 'She was just telling her in her own way to back off.' As usual, Dad was calming the situation, his voice steady and light. 'And the puppy's all right too, aren't you?' He ruffled the fluffy fur on the top of Pup's head.

Mom didn't answer. She walked out of the kitchen and joined the children back on the settee.

Dad took Pup into the living room, leaving Poppy to finish her dinner in peace.

When Poppy had swallowed the last tasty morsel, she plodded into the living room.

Pup scampered over to her. She grumbled, groaned and then barked, 'I'm sorry, Poppy.'

Poppy stopped and belched loudly in her face. 'My dinner. My bowl.' She knew she was being rude, but at that moment, she didn't care.

Pup looked up at her with sorrowful eyes and whimpered, 'Sorry.'

Poppy grunted and walked away, trying to hide the fact that she now felt guilty.

*Wasn't my fault.* She grumbled as she flopped in front of the fireplace. *She needs to be taught a lesson. She was the one trying to steal my dinner. It wasn't my fault. Other dogs would have done much worse. It wasn't my fault…*

But Poppy still felt guilty.

She noticed two rubber bones on the floor, one black and the other pink. Poppy picked up the black bone and balanced it between her front paws. While she began chewing, her teeth squeaking against the rubber, something nudged her. Pup settled beside her, the pink bone between her own front paws. As Poppy chewed, the rubber bone squeaked. As Pup chewed, the pink rubber bone squeaked.

Pup snuggled closer. She gazed up at Poppy, still chewing her rubber bone. Poppy picked her own toy up in her mouth and shook her head from side to side. She dropped it on the floor, looked at it for a few seconds, then pounced. Pup growled and shook her pink bone from side to side too.

Mom chuckled. 'She's copying Poppy, look,' she said.

Jack and Evie giggled.

Poppy was flattered. She thought about life back home with Boxer – the grumpy cat from the neighbouring pub – and the rabbits, squirrels and pigeons. None of them showed any interest in her, or else she was so boisterous she'd frighten them off. Yet, Pup seemed to *want* to be with her. She was even copying everything she did.

Poppy growled softly. Pup dropped her toy and yawned, making her head wobble.

*Now, that's cute*, Poppy thought, watching as the little one curled up beside her, snuggling in as close as she could before falling asleep.

Everyone was watching them. They all had the same soft smile on their faces. Mom even fetched her camera and took a photo of Poppy and Pup together.

Poppy felt tired too. She lowered her head and sighed, then gently rested her chin against Pup. *If the little one wants comforting, it won't hurt to oblige just this once, and besides, it makes everyone else happy too.*

Poppy groaned and closed her eyes. As she drifted off to sleep, she realised that it did feel nice to have someone to cuddle up to. She licked Pup's ears gently and then fell asleep.

# Now What?

Poppy peered her head around Mom and Dad's bedroom door. Bags and suitcases were laid out on the bed.

She watched Mom taking clothes out of the wardrobe and folding them into the case. Mom looked up and saw her standing in the doorway.

'Hello, Poppy.' She smiled then carried on packing. 'It's a boring job but someone's got to do it.'

Poppy barked, 'We're not going home right now, are we?'

'I'm being well organised,' Mom said – as if she understood the meaning behind Poppy's bark. She continued folding trousers, dresses and tops as she spoke. 'I don't fancy packing everything this evening. But have you had a good time?' Now she looked up at Poppy and smiled the big, beaming smile she always gave her when they were having one of their chats.

Poppy sat down. She groaned and growled, 'Yes, but it's gone too quickly.'

Poppy hated the thought of leaving Samson. She'd miss her new friends, the pigs too – and then there was Pup. She was worried what would happen to her once they'd gone home – *that's if she didn't come home with them.* Poppy didn't want to think about that and pushed it to the back of her mind.

Mom dropped the dress she was holding and walked over to Poppy. She crouched down in front of her and cradled Poppy's face in her hands.

'I know what's wrong,' she said, looking into Poppy's eyes. 'You're going to miss Samson, aren't you?'

Poppy leaned forward and licked the tip of Mom's nose. *How does she know what I'm thinking?*

Mom chuckled and folded her arms around Poppy, pulling her gently into a hug.

'Don't be sad, Pops. The holiday isn't over yet, and besides, I've got some news for you.'

Mom leaned back. She was smiling. Her eyes were shining and it looked as if they were smiling too.

*What is it? What's happened?*

The tip of Poppy's tail swished against the carpet. Whatever the news, it must be good. Poppy could sense it.

'You remember Boxer, who lives in the White Stag pub back home?'

Poppy's tail stopped wagging. She narrowed her eyes and grunted.

*Boxer the cat. How could I forget? He hisses and spits every time he sees me.*

'Well…' Mom reached for her phone, which was lying on the bed. She was still smiling, but Poppy had no idea how good news and Boxer went together.

Mom wrapped her arm around Poppy's shoulders, drawing her closer. She held her phone out in front of them both.

'Look,' Mom whispered, her cheek pressed against Poppy's.

Poppy stared at the picture on the screen. It was a kitten. A fluffy ginger and white kitten.

'Cute,' Poppy whined. 'But what's that got to do with Boxer?'

'This little chap's called Teddy,' Mom said softly. 'Rose, the lady from the White Stag Inn, bought him yesterday. He's a companion for Boxer, which means…'

Poppy glanced sideways and saw Mom smiling.

'Meet your new playmate!' she sounded very excited.

Poppy was confused. Maybe she would have shared Mom's excitement before, but here, at Buttercup Farm, she'd finally made good friends. Thinking of Boxer – and now, Teddy – she couldn't imagine their relationship being anywhere near as good.

*Two cats versus one dog.*

Poppy growled.

*Two cats, hissing and spitting.*

She growled again.

'You're going to love Teddy,' Mom continued, undeterred by Poppy's grunts and glares. 'Rose tells me he's so playful and loving. He could be your new best friend. I mean, look…'

Mom held the photo up closer for Poppy to see.

Teddy was adorable. He was lying on his back with his eyes closed. A picture of cuteness and contentment.

Mom nudged her.

'You see this?' She pointed to a stripe of fluffy white fur running down the kitten's belly. 'This is what Rose calls Teddy's lucky stripe.'

Poppy wagged her tail.

*Perhaps Teddy could become a new furriend?*

Mom leaned back and looked into Poppy's face.

'I know you're a gentle-hearted soul, but sometimes you can be a bit boisterous,' Mom chuckled, 'and Dad keeps saying you need a playmate. Now, our neighbours have two cats you can play with! But try a little harder to get along with Boxer – and remember, be gentle with Teddy, he's only a kitten.'

She was right, Dad *was* always saying she needed a playmate. At first, she thought he was joking, but the more he mentioned it, the more Poppy wondered if he was serious.

*A playmate?*

Someone to chase around the garden sounded like fun, unlike the rabbits, birds and squirrels who always ran into the field beyond every time she wanted to play. That always ruined things.

'Anyway, you,' Mom said as she stood up, 'go outside and play with the others. It's more fun than watching me pack.'

Poppy ran outside and saw the others kicking Jack's football around the lawn. Puppy was scampering after it. She looked happy. Her tail was wagging, her eyes were shining and she had the classic golden retriever grin across her face.

Dad tapped the ball to Pup. When she caught it, he picked her up and, taking hold of her little paw, he playfully tapped her on the nose.

'Hey!' Poppy barked. She jumped up onto her back legs. Then, with her front paws pressed against Dad's arm, she prodded Pup with her nose.

Dad laughed. 'All right, Poppy. There's no need to be jealous.' He rubbed her chin, making her jowls wobble.

'Jealous? I'm not jealous!' she barked, then spun around and stood in between Jack and Evie. Dad gently lowered Pup to the ground and the little one scampered over to Poppy.

Poppy felt a strange tug at her heart. *Is this sadness?*

She wondered if Pup's family would get in touch today. She hoped they would, because if not, then what?

Meanwhile, Pup was looking up at her. She looked innocent, trusting – and cheeky.

'Come on,' Pup barked.

Poppy charged towards Dad. When he kicked the ball, everyone ran across the lawn after it, Pup scrambling to keep up.

A gate opened and closed. Poppy turned to see who it was.

'Samson!' she barked and raced towards him.

Poppy couldn't stop howling and barking, especially since he seemed so happy to see her too.

She noticed his gaze shift. As she slowed down, Pup lolloped past her and over to Samson.

*So, was Samson pleased to see me, or Pup?*

The big collie gently sniffed Pup's ears, and Poppy noticed Carol walking towards Dad. She decided to join them, while Samson was fussing over Pup.

By the time Poppy had trotted over to Dad's side, Mom had joined them too. Poppy tried to ignore the sounds of fun and laughter coming from the children, Samson and Pup.

'What time's your boat?' Carol asked.

Dad checked his watch. 'It sets off at about 11.30. We'll need to get going soon.'

'You'll love Dartmouth,' Carol said. 'There are

plenty of shops and the castle is well worth a visit. Oh, and there are lots of ice cream parlours.'

*There was that magic word again – ice cream.*

Poppy barked, 'Yes, please.'

They all looked at her and laughed.

'Not you, Pop. Not this time,' Mom said and rubbed Poppy's chin.

'Dogs are allowed on the boat, though,' Carol said.

Dad shook his head. 'Poppy would hate it. It's not fair putting her through all of that when she can chill out back here with you. That's if you're sure you don't mind?'

Poppy now understood what was happening. Her family were going to go on a boat trip and have ice cream – without her. She didn't like the sound of that.

'You're right,' Carol said. 'Some dogs just don't have sea legs. I've known dogs howl and cry all the way there and back.'

'Well, Poppy's only just started liking the water,' Dad said. 'I doubt she'd be impressed if we took her out in the middle of the sea.'

'Yep, leave me here,' Poppy barked, 'where it's nice and dry.' She then turned tail and ran.

# MORE HOOMAN THAN DOG

It wasn't long before the Robinsons had piled into the car and set off on their way to the harbour. Poppy watched them leave, standing between Pup and Samson. She didn't mind them going without her. *Rather them than me,* she thought and trembled at the idea of the big, rolling sea.

Once the car was out of sight, Carol called to Flo. Her daughter appeared at the gate with Oliver and Olive.

'I'm just going to check on Gracie,' Carol said. Poppy had learned that Gracie was the goat. 'Can you stay here and keep an eye on the dogs?'

'Sure,' Flo said, opening the gate and letting the small dogs trot up the drive.

Poppy glared. She wasn't sure she liked the idea of these two intruding on her turf. She growled.

'What's the matter?' Samson barked. 'It's not Oliver and Olive, is it?'

Poppy shifted from one paw to the other. Pup looked up at her and did the same.

'They don't belong here,' Poppy growled. Pup growled too.

Oliver and Olive mooched up and down the drive, both wearing matching green tartan bandanas. They stayed together, side by side, their bottoms wiggling and their short legs moving rapidly with every stride. Neither seemed bothered by Poppy, Samson and Pup.

Poppy growled again, but Samson gave her a stern look.

'Stop it, Poppy,' he growled. 'Buttercup Farm's *their* home, not yours.'

This made Poppy pause. *Of course it is.* Yet she'd been so used to staying at the cottage that she'd adopted the place as her own.

Meanwhile, the pug and French bulldog ignored them. Poppy realised they must see dogs come and go all the time. Poppy thought it odd that neither of them minded. She'd have hated it.

She watched Olive and Oliver playfully snapping and grunting at each other. It was clear they had a deep affection for one another. This made her feel a little sad, although she couldn't quite understand why.

'Come on,' Samson barked. He ran into the middle of the lawn, to the delight of the pigs who grunted at their canine friends. 'Leave Oliver and Olive to it, Poppy. You'll never see them playing with other dogs.'

Poppy looked from the two dogs – who were still play fighting – to Samson, who was waiting for her.

'Why not?' she growled.

'Because they're happy being spoilt by Carol. Those two are more hooman than dog.'

She remembered what Samson had said back on the beach when she'd been told off by the Yorkshire terrier. He was right – it takes all sorts. It was impossible to be everyone's friend. However, she planned to enjoy every minute with the friends she had made. So, Poppy turned away from Oliver and Olive and joined Samson and the pigs.

As she ran, she heard Pup trying to keep up, her little paws thudding across the grass. Poppy slowed down to let her catch up. The three of them sparred – growling, pawing, jumping and rolling. Behind them, the pigs ran up and down, grunting.

Poppy was the first to get tired. She lay down and

watched Samson and Pup play. For a big dog, he was surprisingly gentle. He tapped Pup's shoulder and nudged her with his nose. He rolled over, but was careful not to roll into her. Meanwhile, Pup was less gentle. She leapt on him, growling and nibbling his paws and his ears. Poppy couldn't believe what she was seeing – Samson was a big softie.

When Pup realised Poppy wasn't joining in, she trotted over and lay down beside her. They watched Flo who was sunbathing on a towel. Oliver and Olive lay on either side of her – both fast asleep.

*Two contented dogs, living together in a home where they want for nothing,* Poppy mused. *Sounds perfect to me.*

Her thoughts turned to Pup.

'What's your mom like?' she growl-howled.

'She looks a lot like you. Her name's Dolly.'

'What about your dad?' Samson growled softly.

Pup shook her head. 'I don't know. All I remember is crawling over my brothers and sisters to get to Mom's milk. It was crowded, but when I got older I had a place of my own.'

Poppy pricked her ears up at the mention of the little one's home.

'What's it like?' Poppy's ears twitched. She was curious and concerned.

Pup wriggled into the grass.

'It's warm and cosy, not as warm and cosy as the cottage, but it's my home and I miss it.'

Samson lay down and crossed his paws.

'Can you tell us about the monster?' he growled. 'You said it roared?'

Poppy noticed Pup stiffen at the mention of the monster. 'Can you remember anything else about it?' Samson barked softly.

'Why do you want to know?' she whined, looking from Samson to Poppy. 'I don't like talking about it. As long as I can stay here with you, the monster won't get me.'

Poppy and Samson looked at each other. It was time for Poppy to explain.

# PUPPY TRAINING CLASS

'We're going back home soon,' Poppy whined, as gently as she could.

Pup's ears flapped to and fro. 'Back home? What do you mean? I thought this was your home.'

Poppy shook her head. 'We're only here for a week. After that, we're going back to our own house.'

Pup stared at her with big, glistening sad eyes. She whimpered.

'And where's that?'

'We live in a house called Childer's View. It's named after the forest across the road.'

'Is it like the wood?'

Poppy nodded. 'Only much bigger.'

'It sounds nice,' Puppy whined, then sighed and looked towards the trees. 'I wish I could go home.'

'Carol's trying her best,' Samson barked. 'She's been phoning the vet and the police to see if there's any news,' he looked at Poppy, 'but so far there's nothing.'

Pup looked crestfallen, but moments later her mood seemed to lift. When she looked up at Poppy and Samson, her eyes were suddenly brighter and more hopeful.

'What if the vet and police never hear anything? Will I stay here?'

'You couldn't,' Samson nodded towards Oliver and Olive, 'they wouldn't make you welcome. Guests staying for a holiday is one thing, but another dog coming to *live* here? Sharing Carol's attention?' He shook his head.

Poppy sighed. *Poor Pup.*

Oliver and Olive were still asleep. Both were snoring loudly, which was amusing Flo as she held her phone out in front of her. Poppy knew what she was doing, she'd seen Mom do it many times before: Flo was filming them.

'Or…' Pup growled, 'maybe I could live somewhere *like* this? If I can't get back home.'

Poppy saw the determination on the little one's face. This puppy wasn't giving up. Poppy admired her positivity, noticing her expression change from deep thought to optimism.

Samson stood up. 'I have an idea,' he said. Poppy

and Pup were all ears. 'There's a possibility that you'll be taken to a rescue centre. I haven't been to one, but from what I've heard, there'll be a lot of other dogs there. That means when someone comes along looking for a dog, you'll need to get yourself noticed. You have to stand out so you'll be picked.'

Poppy's stomach churned. She thought about the other dogs. *Would they be nice to Pup?* She worried about her lying all alone in a small enclosure, just like the ones she'd seen on television, and she worried about the kind of person who would take her. One thing she'd learned over the years was that not every hooman was nice to dogs.

However, despite Poppy's reservations, Pup seemed pleased and excited. She stood in front of Samson and wagged her tail.

'What should I do?' she barked.

Samson looked around. He was thinking hard; Poppy could tell by his stern expression as he looked at everyone.

Poppy's own mind had gone blank. She cussed, wishing she could think of a brilliant plan.

Suddenly, Olive gave a loud snore that turned into a series of grunts. She rolled over, stretching her legs and landing on her belly.

Poppy watched Flo put her phone down and cuddle the pug. Olive glowed in the attention. Then Flo sat up and said, 'Olive, stand.'

Olive slowly stood up.

'Bow.'

Poppy watched Olive lower her head towards the floor, her bottom and curly tail held up to the sun. Flo laughed.

'Good girl.' Flo shuffled on to her knees. 'Now, Olive…' She held something between her thumb and middle finger. Poppy sniffed the air. It was a piece of tasty kibble. Poppy licked her lips as she watched Flo holding it up and say, 'Beg.'

Olive shifted on to her back legs, her eyes fixed on the treat.

'Good girl.' Flo threw the kibble to Olive.

At last, Poppy had an idea…

'Why don't we teach Pup some tricks?' Poppy growled. 'Hoomans love that sort of thing.'

Samson's face lit up. 'Excellent idea!'

Poppy basked in Samson's praise. With her mind still on Olive and her tricks, she said, 'We could teach Pup to *bow* and *beg*?'

Samson's expression changed.

'No. No,' he growled, shaking his head. 'She's a puppy, not a clown.'

Poppy sighed. She should have known Samson wouldn't approve of anything so silly.

'All hoomans like *sit* and *stay*,' he barked.

'And *paw*,' Poppy added, remembering how that always worked for her whenever she wanted an extra treat. This time, she was pleased to see Samson nodding his head in approval.

Pup jumped up. 'OK then, what do I do?'

'First of all, watch Poppy,' Samson barked. He turned to Poppy.

Poppy stood up and waited for his command.

'When a hooman says, "*Sit*," this is what you should do.'

Poppy sat with her back straight, chest out and chin up. 'Like this,' she growled and glanced down at Pup. 'Now, you try.'

When Samson gave the command, Poppy looked on proudly as Pup sat down.

'Very good. Very good,' Samson said and licked Pup's ears.

'Now, for *stay*.' Samson looked at Poppy.

She took a few steps, then turned around. When Samson called, 'Sit', she sat down. Samson then barked, 'Stay.'

As he walked away, Poppy sat perfectly still. She watched him, his tail swinging gently, his smooth coat gleaming in the sun. She looked at Pup and was pleased to see the little one watching her.

'Remember, Pup,' Poppy growled, 'you stay like this until you hear the command.'

Samson turned around and barked, 'Come.'

Poppy jumped to her feet and walked over to Samson. She made sure to walk proudly, to swing her tail and lift her legs – she was doing the Woodville Walk.

'Let me try,' Pup barked.

The little one sat watching Samson. When he turned, Poppy saw Pup fidget. Was she about to run?

Poppy nearly burst with pride when Samson barked, 'Come,' and Pup jumped up and ran to him.

They tried it again, only this time Samson walked farther away. Poppy sat very still, resisting the temptation to remind Pup to stay. She needn't have worried though, Pup knew exactly what to do.

Poppy was so pleased and proud that she ran over to Pup and playfully nudged her. Pup growled and jumped on Poppy, nibbling her ears and her paws, and then swinging from her tail. Poppy rolled on to her back and kicked her legs towards the sky. As she wriggled along the grass, Pup landed on Poppy's belly, her paws draped on either side of her fluffy cream tum.

'Stop it. That tickles!' Poppy growl-howled. Pup growl-howled too.

When Poppy finally managed to wriggle free and roll back on to her paws, she saw Samson watching them. Her heart sank at the thought that she'd shown herself up again. But she couldn't help it. She enjoyed being silly. Then she caught the look on his face and in his eyes. He wasn't annoyed. He was amused.

'Mum.' Flo called.

Carol walked up the drive. She made loud kissing

noises at Olive and Oliver whilst they ran towards her. She scooped them up in her arms and giggled as both dogs licked her face.

'Mom, you'll never guess what I've just seen.' Flo walked over to her mom, waving her phone in the air. They watched the screen and occasionally looked at Poppy, Samson and Pup.

Poppy knew what they were watching. She could hear her own barks and growls, and those of Samson and Pup. Flo had been filming them.

# TREATS!

That afternoon, Carol Briggs spent much of her time on the telephone. Poppy heard her mention the words vet, lost, puppy and re-home again and again. But Carol was talking into her mobile – walking up and down the garden and in and out of the farmhouse – so Poppy couldn't hear the whole conversation.

Pup wanted to play and Poppy was happy to oblige. Playing was her favourite after all. Samson looked at the field where Colin and Bow were working. This time, there was no sad, faraway expression on his face.

'Come and join in, Samson,' Poppy barked as Pup swung from her collar.

But Samson was happy watching Bow. 'Colin's taking me out this evening. Bow's coming too so I can show her where she's going wrong, but…' he raised his chin, his eyes still focused on Bow, Colin and the sheep, 'she's doing well.'

Ever since Poppy had told Samson what Colin's plans were, he had become calmer, relaxed and, Poppy hoped, much friendlier towards Bow.

A car was approaching. Poppy recognised the sound of the engine. She ran to the gate and waited for her family.

The moment Mom climbed out of the car, Poppy jumped and barked, 'Hey! I've missed you!'

She could hardly contain her excitement. She turned and ran up and down the lawn at full speed zoomies. She growled as she went, head down, tongue out. She ran so fast she nearly tripped over her paws.

By the time Dad had parked the car, Poppy was tired out. She stood on the lawn, panting.

Pup trotted over to the children as they climbed out. Evie knelt and opened her arms out to her. Even with Buttercup tucked under her arm, she was still able to cuddle the puppy. Ever since Buttercup had gone missing, Evie had taken her everywhere with her – she wasn't going to risk losing her again. Poppy thought about that day – how distraught Evie had been. It made Poppy wonder how Pup's owners were feeling right now. *They must be beside themselves with worry.*

Carol walked over. She was holding Oliver and Olive, one under each arm.

'Did you have a nice time?' she asked.

Mom told her about their day while Dad took the bags out of the car. Poppy noticed shopping. This got her thinking. *I wonder if they've bought any ice cream?* She licked her lips then trotted over to Dad and pressed her nose into one of the bags.

Dad chuckled. 'Nothing for you in there,' he said. Then he lifted another. 'But as for this one…'

Poppy smelt it at once. *This was even better than ice cream.* Samson now appeared by her side. Judging by the look on his face, he'd smelt it too.

'You might as well give it to her now,' Mom said, then, turning to Carol, 'I remembered you saying that Oliver and Olive are on a strict diet, but we bought a treat for Samson, I hope you don't mind.'

'How lovely!' Carol said. She looked pleased and surprised.

Dad delved into the bag and lifted out two large knucklebones. As soon as he held them aloft, Poppy and Samson sat down at his feet. Poppy stuck her chest out and stayed as still as she could, but she couldn't control the drool that dripped slowly from her jowls. Drip. Drip. And one long trail, glistening in the sunlight and swinging from her mouth.

'Gently,' Dad said as he lowered the treats to them. Samson took the bone carefully and gently. Poppy expected nothing else from such a well-trained dog. However, she was so eager to start gnawing at the bone that she found it hard to be patient. She shuffled on her bottom and licked her lips. Dad lowered it further. She stretched up as far as she could without lifting her bottom off the ground.

'Gently,' Dad said again.

With all the self-control she could muster, Poppy slowly opened her mouth and took the bone. She then trotted to the shady spot beside the barn.

She was pleased to see Samson also preferred to enjoy his special treat alone. He walked away with the bone in his mouth and disappeared through the garden gate that led to the farmhouse.

The knucklebone was delicious. Poppy wrapped her jaws around the meat and bone, her teeth scraping and grinding. She was in her element until she saw Pup. The little one had seen the bone and was coming over.

Poppy froze. She held the bone tightly between her paws. She was about to growl, but Jack called Pup away. If he hadn't been holding a treat for Pup, Poppy was certain she'd have ignored him.

This was bliss. The bone was delicious, and Pup was too happy with her own treat to bother Poppy.

As she gnawed, Poppy listened to Carol tell Mom and Dad how good they'd been in their absence.

'They get along really well.'

Dad leaned against the bonnet and folded his arms, listening to Carol. Evie and Jack chased each other around the garden, both knowing that when a dog has a bone it's best to leave well alone.

'It's like I've always said, that's what Poppy misses,' Dad said.

'Oh, here we go again,' Mom interrupted, rolling her eyes.

'Well, it's true!' Even though Dad had raised his voice, he was also smiling, so Poppy knew there was nothing to worry about. 'Sometimes, Poppy looks fed up.'

'That's the breed,' Mom said, 'they have sad eyes.'

Poppy looked up. *Sad eyes? Do I have sad eyes?*

Carol looked amused at Mom and Dad's playful argument. 'I've spoken to the vet and I've called the police station again. Still nothing,' she said.

Poppy saw the smiles fade from Mom and Dad's faces.

# TEAMWORK

'So, now what?' Dad asked.

Carol shook her head slowly. 'The vet was saying that with the puppy not being microchipped, and no one coming forward, there's little else we can do, unless…' she looked at Mom and Dad.

The tone of Carol's voice left Poppy in no doubt as to her meaning. She stopped gnawing her bone and lifted her head. There was no way she wanted Pup coming home with them.

Carol was smiling at her pawrents. Dad was now smiling at Mom. But Mom looked at both of them and shook her head,

'Oh no,' she said, much to Poppy's relief, 'it wouldn't be fair on Poppy.'

'It'll be great for Poppy!' Dad said, raising his voice slightly, 'I keep telling you…'

But Mom still shook her head. 'Look what happened yesterday when the puppy went near Poppy's dinner. And I've seen how Poppy looks sometimes.' Dad opened his mouth to speak but Mom continued. 'At times she doesn't seem her usual happy self. I'm worried she'll get jealous, she's used to being the only one and to suddenly have to share everything will be too much of a shock for her. I don't think she'd take to another dog.'

Carol nodded. 'I can see your point.' She looked at her own dogs then said, 'I have to make sure neither of these is left out. Both are treated equally.' She planted a kiss on the top of each of their heads.

Dad smiled sadly. Poppy could see he'd accepted defeat.

Now the panic was over, Poppy returned to her bone. Yet, she still kept an ear open, eavesdropping on their conversation, just in case there was any more talk of Pup coming to stay with them.

'I've had a chat with Ann Powell. She's the lady who runs the local golden retriever rescue centre,' Carol said. 'She's agreed to take Pup. It's like she said, a puppy isn't going to be so difficult to rehome.'

'Perfect!' Mom said.

Dad nodded and looked at Pup. The little one was oblivious to their conversation but Poppy listened to every word.

*That's that then. Pup is going to a rescue home for golden retrievers – unless her owners finally get in touch.*

'So,' Dad said, 'did the dogs get along well?'

'You're not going to believe this,' Carol said, 'but Samson and Poppy were training her.'

Mom and Dad laughed.

'No, honestly,' Carol said, 'you should have seen them. OK, so maybe not exactly training her, but if I didn't know better I'd say that's what they were doing.'

Mom giggled, 'I can just see it now, Poppy barking, "Sit!"'

'Hold on,' Carol said. 'I'll be right back. I've got to show you this.'

Mom and Dad were talking quietly to each other and the children were now chatting to the pigs. When Pup had finished her treat, she stood up and looked around. She looked at Poppy and ran towards her.

Poppy froze for a second then grabbed her bone. She stared at Pup and this seemed to do the trick.

'Sorry, Poppy. Shall I leave you alone?'

Poppy nodded. *She catches on quickly,* she thought, feeling proud of the little one.

'You'll be able to eat one of these when you're older,' Poppy whined – realising that explaining to Pup made her feel less guilty.

As Poppy returned to her bone, Pup ran over to Evie and Jack. Poppy heard her trying to make conversation with the pigs. *Good luck with that…*

Carol came back with Flo. Poppy guessed Oliver and Olive had been given some delicious treat back at the house.

'Look at this,' Carol said. Flo held her phone up to Mom and Dad.

Everyone was quiet as they watched the screen. Poppy heard the same growls and barks as before. She looked up and caught Mom and Dad's eyes. They both seemed shocked.

'Well I never.' Mom's words were slow and quiet.

'You wouldn't believe it, would you?' Carol said, grinning.

Dad looked from Poppy to Pup and said, 'They do make a good team.'

Mom hummed in agreement, then said, 'Yes, I guess they do. But I still think getting another dog is a bad idea.'

# WHAT ABOUT PUP?

While the Robinsons ate fish and chips, Poppy and Pup tucked into their meal of meat and vegetables. This time, Poppy observed, Pup knew her place and left Poppy's food alone.

Poppy hungrily slurped and scoffed her dinner. Now and then she looked over at Pup, just to check. Each time she found the little one busily tucking into her food too. She couldn't help but be impressed by the way the little one ate; she had a hearty appetite.

*That's my girl.*

As everyone ate, Dad talked about the traffic. It was a bank holiday weekend, which meant the roads would be busy.

'I've got a good mind to set off tonight,' he said, then bit into his chip butty. Poppy stared at the melting butter oozing between the bread crusts. Pup stared too, but she decided to go one step further and rest her chin on his lap.

Dad smiled and tickled her ears. Poppy noticed a flicker of sadness in his eyes. She tilted her head. *What's wrong?*

Despite her efforts, Pup didn't get any of Dad's chip butty. Poppy didn't think she would. In all her four years, she'd never been allowed chips let alone a chip butty – *I bet it would be nice, though.*

'We could go tonight,' Mom said. 'All the packing's done.'

But Jack and Evie were not happy.

'I don't want to leave early!' Jack protested, his mouth set into a firm line.

'Me neither,' Evie cried, 'I want to stay.'

'We'd only miss an evening watching TV,' Dad said.

'And if we do go in the morning, your dad will want to leave early to miss the worst of the traffic,' Mom added.

Evie frowned. 'What time?'

Dad leaned back in his chair. 'Well, on a good run it takes four hours, but you can double that for a bank holiday, and…' he looked at Jack, seeing his son was about to argue, 'and there's no way I'm sitting in the car for eight hours. So, I'd want to set off at half-past five.'

'In the morning!' Jack looked horrified.

'Yes, in the morning,' Dad said, smiling.

Poppy knew there was no way the children would get up that early, especially Evie – she liked her bed too much.

Jack and Evie looked at each other, then sighed and looked down at their plates.

'OK,' Jack mumbled.

'Right then,' Dad said brightly. He pushed his chair back and stood up. 'After I've washed up we'll have a drink, and then I'll get the car ready.'

'So, that's it then,' Poppy groaned, 'we're heading back today.' Part of her was pleased. She didn't fancy the idea of being cooped up in the car for eight hours, but this had been the best holiday ever and she didn't want it to end.

'What about the puppy?' Jack said, his face downcast. Poppy noticed his bottom lip begin to wobble, as did his voice.

'Oh no. Puppy!' Evie cried. She jumped off her chair and knelt down beside Pup. She wrapped her arm around her neck and kissed the top of her head. Pup looked confused. Poppy sighed. Explaining would be her next job – and she wasn't looking forward to it.

Mom stood up and sighed. She held on to the back of the chair and looked down at the children.

'I told you this was going to happen. Didn't I say not to get too attached?' Mom looked from Jack to Evie.

'Why can't we keep her? She's practically ours anyway,' Jack said.

'Because, Jack, she's not our dog.' Mom leaned over her chair. Even though she spoke softly, Poppy could hear the tension in her voice. It seemed that Mom had been dreading this moment too, although Poppy wasn't sure if it was for the same reason.

'But Mom, I don't want to leave her,' Evie cried against Pup's ear.

Pup looked at Poppy with wide, bewildered eyes. 'What's going on?' she whined.

Poppy brushed her nose over Pup's face.

'See?' Evie cried. 'Poppy doesn't want her to go either.' She stroked the long, soft fur on Poppy's chest and sobbed.

'Oh, Evie,' Mom sighed, 'no one ever said we'd keep her. You both knew from the start that we were only looking after her until someone claimed her, or until it was time for us to go home.'

Poppy walked to the top of the stairs. 'Pup, let's go outside,' she barked.

'I think Poppy needs to go out,' Dad said, then walked down the stairs.

'Pup, come on,' Poppy barked. She stood and waited, seeing the confused puppy standing beside Evie, her ears flapping in response to Evie's cries.

Pup wriggled out of Evie's arms and lolloped towards Poppy. They ran down the stairs, both eager to be outside and away from all the tears and sadness.

The pigs were waiting to greet them. They pressed their snouts through the fence and grunted happily. 'Poppy… Pigs… Poppy… Pigs…'

It cheered Poppy up to see them. She and Pup walked over and gruff-barked at them. No one knew what the others were saying, but it didn't matter. Instead, the four of them ran up and down the fence together.

As they ran, Poppy heard Colin whistle. It was in the distance and Poppy knew where it was coming from. She looked across the pigsty and hedges to the field beyond. Samson was running across the field with Bow. The sheep must have already been herded because except for the collies and Colin, the field was empty. Poppy watched Samson and Bow playing.

*What a change.* Poppy thought. *He's much happier now.*

It seemed Pup had tired the pigs out. Poppy watched them grunting softly, their snouts pressed into the ground. Then, finally, they plodded away, their curly tails reminding Poppy of Olive-the-pug.

Pup's eyes were everywhere, her tail wagging, ears twitching, at every sound, whether loud or soft. She was alert, and she was happy.

'Thank you!' Poppy barked to the pigs.

'Yes. Thank you!' Pup squeaked-barked too.

But Poppy wasn't thanking them for their game. She was showing her gratitude for cheering them up. A distraction from the tearful scene earlier was what they both needed.

'What shall we do now, Poppy?' she barked.

Poppy loved Pup's brown sparkling eyes and her small white teeth and pink tongue that formed the classic golden retriever grin.

She remembered Mom's earlier comment about their breed having sad eyes. Maybe that was true, but right now, Pup's eyes looked far from sad.

*Do I have sad eyes?* Poppy wondered. She thought about her life back home. *I suppose I do, especially when Boxer, that bad-tempered cat, hisses and spits at me. And then there's the rabbits, birds and squirrels who always run away whenever I want to play…*

'What's wrong, Poppy?'

She shook herself from her thoughts as Pup waited for her answer. *That's a good question*, Poppy thought, *what is wrong?*

Jack and Evie walked outside. They both still looked upset. Jack kicked the ball against the wall while Evie sat at the table with Buttercup.

'What's up with everyone?' Pup whined.

'Come on,' Poppy barked, spotting two rabbits running into the wood.

Pup trotted and skipped ahead. Poppy howled softly. She'd miss the little swish of that tail, those sparkling eyes, even the feel of Pup's sharp teeth chewing her ears. She thought about their games – Pup swinging from Poppy's collar or her ears, not to mention their tugs-of-war with the socks. Then, there were the nights curled up together, Pup's small, warm body pressed against hers. There was no question about it, Poppy was going to miss the little scamp.

# THE LEGEND OF CHILDER'S FOREST

Poppy and Pup walked into the wood. They pushed through tall ferns and nettles.

'Do you have rabbits in the forest back home?' Pup barked.

'Yes, lots of them. And squirrels, birds, foxes, badgers and deer.'

'Deer? What's that?'

'They're bigger than the other woodland animals, but they're no danger, so long as you don't get too close, especially when they're with their young. Then there's the stag.'

'The what?'

'The stag. I've only seen him once. He's big and white, and has long antlers, like claws.'

'He sounds scary,' Pup said, trembling.

Poppy whined softly. 'As long as you're no threat, he's fine. Dad calls him the Legend of Childer's Forest.'

'Childer's Forest?' Pup sounded both fascinated and scared.

'That's the name of the forest back home. The pub near us is called The White Stag after him.'

'I wish I could see him.'

'Not many do. I was lucky once, but I haven't seen him since.'

'I'm going to miss this wood,' Pup whined, gazing at the trees and bushes.

Poppy felt an ache in her chest. She felt like whining too.

'How did you get here, Pup?'

The puppy shook her head. 'I don't remember. One minute I was curled up in bed, the next I heard the monster.' She shivered.

Poppy was determined to get to the bottom of this mystery. Pup's home, her comfy bed, the mysterious monster and then ending up in the wood – it just didn't add up.

Poppy stopped. She was going nowhere until she had answers. 'So, you were in your bed…'

Pup nodded. 'Yes, I was curled up with my toy. I'd just been fed so I was feeling tired.'

'Who fed you?'

243

'My hooman.'

'Ah!' Poppy was getting somewhere at last. 'And what's your hooman's name?'

'I don't know.'

'What does your hooman look like?'

Pup paused. 'I don't remember,' she groaned.

'Was your hooman nice to you?'

'Oh yes, he fed me and gave me water.'

'A-ha…so your hooman is a man! What about your mom?'

'She went away, like my brothers and sisters…' Pup looked into the distance, 'I guess we were sent to our new homes.'

Poppy was confused. 'Are you saying this wood is your new home?'

Pup shook her head firmly. 'Oh no. My home smells of Mom and has my toy. It's comfy and cosy and it's where I feel safe.'

'Until the monster came along?'

'Yes.'

Poppy mulled things over. There was a lot to take in and try to make sense of. Unfortunately, she was still none the wiser. But their time at Buttercup Farm was running out and – as was usual for Poppy – the more her mind digested information, the more curious she became. The uncertainty surrounding Pup made her feel anxious and afraid. She'd grown to care for her and her welfare which resulted in the need to know just what had happened.

'So, Pup…' Poppy had the little one's full attention. 'I know you don't like talking about this, but we need to know exactly what happened. From the moment the monster woke you, to the moment I found you here.'

Pup nodded.

'So…' Poppy prompted.

Pup took a deep breath. 'At first, I heard the monster's growls,' she trembled at the memory, 'and I lay still. I was hoping it would go away, but then I saw it. If I hadn't moved quickly, it would have seen me. I had no choice but to leave my lovely home. It was dark. I couldn't see where I was going, but I knew I had to get away.'

Poppy nodded. 'Yes. Yes. Go on,' she growled.

But Pup shook her head. 'It was dark. I don't know where I went. I stopped when I couldn't hear the monster. I was frightened,' she said, trembling. Poppy comforted her with licks and nuzzles.

'Can you tell me anything else? What did the monster look like?'

Pup scrunched her face as she thought.

Poppy held her breath, hoping the little one would come up with a vital clue to help solve the mystery.

'I wonder if it was an animal from another farm. A cow maybe? Or a bull?' But before Pup could answer,

245

Poppy answered her own question, 'No, it doesn't sound like either of those.'

'Bulls? Cows?' Pup frowned, tipping her head from side to side.

*Maybe an animal escaped from the local zoo, like a dhole?* Poppy wondered. *But, as Samson said, the likelihood of that was slim; besides, the hoomans would know about that by now, it would have been in all the local newspapers and websites.*

Poppy thought of every animal she knew. She thought about the forest back home. The deep calls echoing through the trees. Sometimes, the sounds made her tremble. They were eerie, frightening even…

'Did the monster have antlers?' Poppy growled, slowly. Seeing the confused look on Pup's face, she explained, 'They're like claws – long, curved and sharp, except they grow from your head, not your paws.'

Then a look of realisation dawned on Pup's face.

'Yes! Big, big claws sticking up.' She barked, shivering.

Poppy comforted the frightened puppy with more licks and nuzzles against her golden ears. Now Poppy was sure.

'Pup, I think you saw a stag.'

'Like the one in your forest?'

Poppy nodded. 'And you were right to move out of its way. It might have charged into you. For the stag to be calling that loudly, it must have been angry.'

'It was *very* loud Poppy, and its antlers were *huge*.'

'A stag…' Poppy tried to imagine the sight. The brief glimpse she'd caught of the Legend of

Childer's Forest had filled her with fear, surprise and awe. But to see a stag close up – that must have been tremendous. Yet, to a small pup it would have been terrifying.

Pup looked around at the trees, hedges, ferns and tall grass. 'So there are stags in here? In this wood? With us now?'

'Yes…' Poppy's growl trailed away as her mind wandered back to the day she arrived at Buttercup Farm.

'But this is what's been nagging me,' Poppy said as she looked around. 'When we arrived, I remember Mom panicking because I was heading into the wood. Dad told her not to worry because it's enclosed so I couldn't get out.'

Pup looked at her. Poppy could tell she hadn't grasped what she was trying to say.

'If I couldn't get out, then how did you get in?'

Pup barked loudly.

'There was an opening, so I went through.'

Poppy stared at the trees. She narrowed her eyes…

Suddenly a thought flashed into her mind – like a light being switched on in the middle of the night.

'An opening? Like a door?' she barked.

Poppy didn't wait for an answer. She stood up and walked down the uneven, narrow path.

'Come on,' she barked, 'we need to find this opening, room, door or whatever it is you found.'

# IN SEARCH OF ANSWERS

Poppy saw the fence through the trees. It was tall and made of wood and it stretched as far as she could see.

Pup followed Poppy, who was sniffing the ground and cautiously making her way through wild twisted brambles, branches and leaves.

Some parts of the fence were hidden behind overgrown bushes and nettles. Still, Poppy tried to get as close as possible, pushing ferns aside with her nose and lowering her head to part the tangle of matted overgrowth. But there was no sign of a door.

Poppy walked further and further, following the panels. The fence seemed to go on forever, until changing direction and leading back to the farm.

Poppy looked back to check Pup was still with her.

'Is any of this familiar?' she growled, looking at the second fence that stretched into the distance.

When Pup didn't answer, Poppy turned and saw her staring at a tree.

'Pup? are you OK?'

She was deep in thought, but then turning to Poppy, she barked, 'When I saw you I decided to stay here and watch. I was trying to pluck up the courage to say hello.'

Poppy's mind was in overdrive. She contemplated everything. An angry stag. Pup's cosy home. It was dark. A doorway in the fence…

But there was no door. There was just panel after panel stretching as far as she could see. Like Carol Briggs had said, the wood was fully enclosed.

'Come on,' Poppy said, 'we'll keep looking.'

They continued walking as close to the fence as they could. After a while, Poppy started to lose hope.

'Are you sure it was a door?' Poppy growled. 'Can you remember anything about it? Its colour? What it felt like? Did it have a latch or a doorknob?'

Pup stared at her.

*I've lost her*, Poppy realised from the bemused look on the puppy's face. She sighed, trying not to lose patience but feeling that all plausible suggestions were running out.

Poppy looked around. 'There's got to be an opening…' she grumbled to herself. 'There's got to be somewhere you came through…'

'It was dark, Poppy. I didn't have time to look properly. I just saw it and dived.'

They pressed on, wading through brambles and bracken, walking around trees and past rabbit burrows and badger setts.

The smell of rabbit was strong. Poppy pushed her nose under a large overgrown bush and found a burrow. She guessed it was home to about four rabbits. The urge to dig was almost overwhelming, but she resisted. The last thing she wanted to do was disturb them or, even worse, frighten them.

Poppy stopped. It was so sudden that Pup stumbled into her.

'What is it? Is it the stag?' Puppy whined.

'Pup. When you say you dived through the door, what do you mean exactly?'

Pup sat down. She thought for a moment, then barked, 'It was darker there, so I thought if I dived down, then the monster wouldn't see me.'

Poppy frowned. 'You dived down?'

Pup nodded.

'Like digging a tunnel down?'

Pup's face brightened. 'Yes, I went down, but I didn't dig.'

Poppy was on to something.

'OK,' she barked slowly and quietly, 'so you didn't dig, but you still went down, like through a hole already dug?'

Pup jumped to her feet. 'Yes! Yes!' she barked.

Poppy gave the rabbit burrow one last sniff before carrying on. As they walked alongside the fence, Poppy kept her nose to the floor, scared that she might walk past the hole that had been Pup's way in.

After a short while, Pup started to bark.

'Poppy! The tree! I recognise that tree!'

A tall, thin tree had fallen and was leaning against another. Pup ran over to it. Poppy followed. She tried not to build her hopes up but this was the closest they'd been to solving the mystery.

In a few short hours, Poppy would be in the car with the Robinsons on their way back home. When that happened, all chances of discovering what happened to Pup would be lost forever.

Poppy felt that strange ache in her chest again. She felt like whining – but why?

Pup leapt on to the trunk of the fallen tree and looked around. Her head turned sharply as she scanned the area.

Meanwhile, Poppy stood and watched, giving the little one time to think. They were running out of time and Poppy was struggling to stay calm. She couldn't bear to say goodbye to Pup and still not know where she came from. She couldn't bear to think of the puppy's family still out there, missing her. And she couldn't bear the thought of going back home and not knowing where Pup would end up.

'Poppy! I think I know! I think it might be somewhere around…' Pup leapt off the tree and ploughed through a tunnel of bracken.

Poppy lost sight of her. She panicked and charged after her.

'Pup! Pup, where are you?' she barked.

'Over here.'

Poppy followed the sound of her barks and soon saw the tall grass and nettles swaying as the puppy charged through.

To her relief, she found Pup standing in front of the fence. She was panting heavily and, judging by the look on her face, she had found something.

Grass and twigs were stuck in the little one's ears. She looked back at Poppy with bright eyes and a fabulous goldie grin.

'Poppy. I can't believe it. Look, I've found it!'

# THE MONSTER

Poppy stepped forward. There was a small hole beneath the fence. It was too small for her, but a puppy could easily squeeze through.

Pup dived for the hole and was about to disappear inside when there was an almighty roar. She spun around and cowered behind Poppy.

Poppy shrank back. *That is no stag.*

She could feel the little one's body trembling. It was no use barking instructions; Pup would never hear her above the monster's roars. Poppy tried to hide her fear. The last thing she wanted was Pup to know she was afraid too. She had to be brave. The roars continued from behind the fence, and they were getting louder. She looked left and right for another way out, but there was none. Poppy took a step towards the hole.

It was no good she would have to make the hole bigger. The monster was close. Its roars vibrated through her body. It was terrifying. She was frightened. But there was nothing else for it. Poppy had to dig.

Poppy dug and dug. Her heart raced. Her legs trembled.

When she stopped to catch her breath, she heard Pup calling her. Poppy didn't answer. She was too busy listening to that roar. It was strangely familiar.

Poppy had met all sorts of animals back at the safari park, but none of them sounded like this – so where had she heard that roar before?

Perhaps it wasn't at the safari park. Maybe she'd heard that sound in Childer's Forest? Or in the park? Or even out on the fields back home?

Then it dawned on her. Everything clicked into place.

Poppy plunged headfirst into the hole. Dirt flew out behind her. She pushed, scratched, and wriggled through the hole and under the fence.

As she stuck her head out the other side, she was just in time to see the monster making its way off into the distance. Poppy gulped. Her throat felt dry and tight. Her hunch was right.

A tractor was driving slowly down the road. Held above the vehicle were huge claw-like spikes suspended from two thick metal arms.

Poppy scrambled out of the hole. She watched Colin drive the tractor until it disappeared out of sight around a bend in the road.

'Pup. Come on out. It's all right,' Poppy barked.

She heard Pup scrambling through the hole, and then her little golden head appeared. She peered from beneath the fence panel, her eyes looking left and right.

'Come on,' Poppy barked softly, 'it's OK.'

Pup crawled out and stood beside her.

'Where's the stag? I can still hear it.'

Poppy explained. What Pup had thought was a monster – and what she'd mistaken as a stag – was actually Colin Briggs' tractor.

'So, it wouldn't have eaten me?' Pup growled.

Poppy shook her head.

'But that noise!'

'Dad calls it an engine.'

'And those eyes?'

'The tractor's headlights.'

'And those claws?'

'I've seen farmers use it on their fields, it's called a plough. They're not claws.'

'So, it's not a monster? It's not an angry stag, and it wouldn't hurt me?'

'Well…' Poppy shook her head. Pieces of twig and weeds fell out of her fur. 'A tractor would hurt you if you stood in the way. But it's not a monster.'

Pup stared at the empty road.

'So, now we know who – or what – the monster is,' Poppy barked as she walked alongside the road, making sure to keep close to the fence, 'now, we need to find your home.'

Pup walked beside her. They sniffed the tall grass but smelt nothing out of the ordinary.

Poppy didn't want to walk too far for fear of becoming lost. She stopped and looked around for another farm or house. There was nothing except hedges, fields and a road sign. Poppy knew the word on the sign; she'd seen it many times before.

The sign read, Devon.

Poppy looked at it and sighed. *I love Devon.* This was by far the best holiday she'd ever had.

Just then, something else caught Poppy's eye. It peeked out from behind the signpost. It was something that, in Poppy's view, looked out of place.

'Wait there a minute, Pup,' she barked, and then went to investigate.

# HOME

Poppy frowned.

*Some thoughtless person has thrown their rubbish into the hedge.*

Yet, Poppy caught a familiar scent. It was Pup's smell and also the faint hint of another.

She took a closer look. It was a ripped, tatty cardboard box with an old, stained newspaper folded up inside. Tucked into a corner was a faded, scruffy toy. It was the toy that smelt different. Poppy sniffed. She was certain that was the scent of Pup's mom.

Poppy whined as the realisation dawned on her. This was where Pup came from. And as if to confirm her suspicions, Pup ran over to the box and dived inside.

'You've found it!' she barked, then rolled on top of the toy and newspaper. Poppy was amazed at how happy Pup seemed to be back inside the tatty old box.

'Thank you, Poppy,' Pup whined and howled, then buried her face in the soft toy, snorting and sniffing.

The little one was deliriously happy, yet Poppy felt sad. She thought about her own puppyhood back at Woodville Retrievers. Happy memories flooded back of being with her mom and siblings in a room full of colourful rosettes. She remembered the lady's kind face and the hugs and kisses she gave. She remembered the big fireplace with its roaring fire and her bed, filled with toys and shredded paper.

Now, here she stood with Pup, who was ecstatic to be reunited with a tatty box, a stained newspaper and an old toy.

'But, I don't understand,' Poppy gruffed. 'If this is your home, where are your hoomans?'

Pup looked up at her and she tilted her head. 'I don't know. I just remember being carried here. The man patted my head and said something like, *Stay here.* Then he hurried away, but it was too dark to see where he went.'

'Think, Pup, think,' Poppy barked, although she already had a good idea about what had happened that night. 'What did you hear straight afterwards? A car? Voices?'

'Oh, yes!' Pup jumped up and down, excited to have remembered more about that fateful night. 'A car.

I heard a car. A door closed and then I heard it drive away.' Her barks of excitement faded, as did the sparkle in her eyes. The truth had now dawned on her too.

Poppy's chest ached, and this time she whined – only now she knew why – it was sadness, sympathy and an overwhelming need to protect. She loved Pup and there was nothing she wanted more in the world than to raise her as her own.

But what was she going to do? Even though she now knew no family was looking for Pup, there was a golden retriever rescue centre ready to take her in.

Pup would be fine, Poppy was sure of it. The centre wouldn't rehome her to just anyone. But Poppy didn't want her to go!

Poppy wanted Pup to come home with them – to be a Robinson, to share her toys, her treats and… her family.

She was so wrapped up in her thoughts and concerns for Pup that she hadn't realised anyone was approaching until she heard someone call her name.

She looked around and saw her family. She started to wag her tail, but then she saw that Evie and Jack were crying and Mom's face was flushed.

Poppy whined. *What's happened?*

# DEVON

Dad walked at the front of the group. He didn't look too happy, but when Poppy walked towards him, his face softened into a smile. He held his arms open and she ran to him.

'What are you doing out here?' he said, whisking her up in his arms. He buried his face in the fur on her neck.

Mom and the children caught them up. Poppy felt them stroking and hugging her.

*What's the matter with everyone?*

'How did she get out?' Mom said and looked back towards the gate.

Poppy then realised how close they were to Buttercup Farm. The gate to the cottage was just a little further up the road – she could see it clearly now.

Dad lowered Poppy to the ground, but before she could join Pup, Mom and Dad knelt beside her.

'You gave us a fright, Poppy,' Dad said softly, his hand stroking her back. Poppy was glad to see her pawrents were now smiling.

'We thought we'd lost you and the puppy.' Mom's voice shook and her lips trembled.

Suddenly, Jack and Evie called out, 'Mom. Dad. Come here, quick!'

Jack and Evie were sitting on the floor beside Pup and the box. Poppy followed Mom and Dad. She sensed their sadness as they realised the situation.

'Poor little mite,' Dad said quietly. He picked Pup up and cradled her in his arms.

'It looks like someone dumped her here,' Mom said as she ran her hand gently over Pup's face.

Pup wriggled to be free. When Dad let her go, she lolloped over to Poppy.

'So, she hasn't got a family?' Jack said. 'But why? Why would someone just leave her?'

Mom shook her head. Her eyes looked sad, and she

chewed her bottom lip. Poppy guessed that was to stop it from trembling.

'Unfortunately, there are people out there who do things like that. Maybe they couldn't afford to keep her, or pets aren't allowed where they live. Who knows?'

'Thank goodness Poppy found her,' Evie said.

'Yes. Thank goodness.' Poppy could hear the wobble in Dad's voice.

Pup scampered back to her box and Poppy followed.

'Do you know what this means, Pup?'

The joy and excitement left Pup's face. She nodded. 'It means I haven't got a home.'

Poppy climbed into the box beside her. It was a bit snug, but she managed to squeeze in. She wondered how long it had been since Pup was cuddled by her mom.

Pup snuggled against her. She fidgeted. 'It's not as comfortable as I remember it,' she groaned.

Mom clicked her tongue and called, 'Poppy. Puppy.'

Mom took a photograph of them squeezed inside the box beneath the Devon road sign. She looked at the photo on the screen and smiled.

'That's lovely, look,' she said and held the camera up for everyone to see. 'I've just thought of the perfect name. We could call her Devon.'

She smiled at Jack and Evie, who were dumbstruck. While the children gasped and spluttered with shock, Mom's eyes sparkled. Her lips were no longer trembling.

'I'll speak to Carol,' Mom said. 'I think she'll be

pleased. I get the feeling she wanted us to keep her anyway.'

Dad picked Devon up while Mom fastened Poppy's lead to her collar.

'Come on, Devon,' Dad said as they walked back to the cottage. 'Let's take you home.'

# Acknowledgements

This book was written during the height of lockdown. I spent every day walking my dogs – or *my girls* as I like to call them – around the forest. It was so quiet. No one was in sight. Except for the multitude of birds twittering in the treetops above, we were all alone. It was very peaceful and perfect for losing myself in my thoughts. Ideas sprang to mind. Images of scenes unfolded whilst my girls chased each other around the trees. Despite it being lockdown and a very worrying time, the weeks we spent in the forest were fantastic. Those scenes where Poppy and Devon are searching the woods was what I saw those days while walking along our deserted woodland walks.

Samson, the proud and handsome border collie, was based upon my auntie and uncle's dog, Ricky. Sadly, he passed away over thirty years ago, but I remember him well. He was – and still is – the best-trained dog I'd ever known. He was devoted to his master – my uncle, who'd done a fantastic job training him. I remember my dad saying that Ricky would let you into the house, but you'd never get out again – unless my uncle was there to call Ricky away. I remember he was a big collie – but then I was only little, so he would have seemed much bigger than he really was! We – my dad especially – loved

Ricky so much that we ended up having border collies of our own [hence the book I wrote entitled *Tammy and Willow*, which, although purely fiction, is dedicated to the collies we had.]

I couldn't make this acknowledgement without mentioning Biteford Farm in North Devon. This is where I had the inspiration for Buttercup Farm. Many aspects are fiction, though, such as the monster in the nearby forest (thankfully), Olive and Oliver (although wouldn't it be wonderful to meet these two charming characters!), The Briggs family, to name just a few. But the pigs and the cottage are very much what I remember about that lovely Whitsun week spent there. It was one of Poppy's first holidays, and she did indeed enjoy running along the fence while the pigs trotted beside her, grunting merrily. She loved playing football on the large lawn and lazing at the top of the stairs, where she could also peep out of the window at the other farm animals below. Thank you, Angela and Philip, for a wonderful and memorable holiday. One day, I should like to return only this time with my goldie, Devon too.

A huge thank you also goes out to my fantastic editor, Antonia Prescott, who is always a joy to work with. The team at Matador Books, for all your support and another enjoyable experience working with you on this, my third published book. I'd also like to thank the team at LitPR and The Author School. Helen Lewis and Abiola Bello, your words of wisdom and friendship are priceless, and I'm so glad to have met you. Also, a big thank you to Fai Jeavons; thank you for proofreading the manuscript and being a good friend. I also want to thank my son, Nathan, for designing the book cover – it's even better than I'd imagined. It's good to know there is a fantastic team behind me, and with Nathan, Antonia, Fai, Matador, LitPR and the Author School Society, that is precisely what I have; thank you so much.

Last but definitely not least, my heartfelt thanks go to my family and friends. You've always been there, right by my side, listening to me wittering on about my books, plots – and my girls, of course. Your support means the world, and I'd never have gotten this far without it. A huge thank you to my cousin, Janet Moss, for supplying me with some lovely photos of Ricky, which enabled me to create the images of Samson that you see in this book. I'd especially like to thank my dear friends – who are more like family, Sian and Lee. Also, my parents, my children, Nathan and Becki and my husband, Mark.

And…a big thank you goes to you, my readers. I hope you enjoyed Poppy Loves Devon. After writing the debut about Poppy in *Poppy on Safari*, it seemed a natural progression to write a sequel featuring her sister, Devon. There may be more adventures starring the two goldies in time. It's great fun writing about them. My head and my journals are brimming with more adventures for them to experience. But in the meantime, thank you all and take care.

This book is printed on paper from sustainable sources managed under the Forest Stewardship Council (FSC) scheme.

It has been printed in the UK to reduce transportation miles and their impact upon the environment.

For every new title that Matador publishes, we plant a tree to offset $CO_2$, partnering with the More Trees scheme.

For more about how Matador offsets its environmental impact, see www.troubador.co.uk/about/